അ ഏ

Like four shadows we darted from monument to monument as the darkness grew thicker. Then we were in woods again, dark woods. I could hardly see Robert's faded blue shirt ahead of me. In the muggy night air, a sticky dampness coated my skin, and the ringing buzz of cicadas sounded through the trees. Iris Elizabeth clutched the back of my dress and stumbled along behind me. Off to the left, a loud yelp and thrashing about instantly silenced the cicadas. We froze and listened to the far-off sounds of crickets and a frog.

"Must have been a couple of dogs," Robert said.

We had just started moving again when a faint whiff of skunk reached us.

"*Whew*," James said. "Glad we didn't run into that fellow."

"*Ooo*," Iris Elizabeth said. "Was that a skunk?"

"Sure was," James said. "Somebody's dog got a blast."

I wasn't near as worried about skunks as I was about where to put my bare feet. Every little rustle of grass or leaves reminded me of snakes. Daddy always said, "Snakes are more afraid of you than you are of them." Robert was probably scaring off all the snakes. But who knew about snakes?

"Here's the last fence," James whispered. "Don't make a sound. Forest Hill has a night watchman."

ഛ ഏ

Grace E. Howell

True Friends

For Amanda,
May all your friends
be true.
Grace E. Howell
11/05/05

Echelon Press

Echelon Press
56 Sawyer Circle #354
Memphis, TN 38103
www.echelonpress.com

Copyright © 2005 by Grace E. Howell
ISBN: 1-59080-420-1
Library of Congress Control Number: 2005927262

First Echelon Press paperback printing: August 2005

Cover Art © Nathalie Moore
2005 Arianna Best In category Award

Printed in USA

Dedication

For Grace, Stella, all the Bolly girls and boys, and Annie Belle Davis.

Acknowledgement

Thanks to my family's support, their encouraging words, and their willingness to answer all my questions, TRUE FRIENDS is what it is. Joyce and Kathy especially have been with me all the way from the first idea to the last word.

.

Chapter One

Memphis, Tennessee – July 1918

Miz Lizzie was always advising Mama to start making a lady out of me. To avoid her sharp eyes, I slunk through the tall Johnson grass as long as I could before I ran across the road toward home. The sky had darkened, and thunder rolled in the distance. Zipping around the house to the back, I hoped to wash off at the pump before Mama saw me. She'd have my hide for coming home covered with drying brown clay. But there she was, sitting on the back porch, snapping beans.

"Annie Lou Davis, *where* have you been?" she asked.

When I started to answer, my mud mask cracked around my mouth and along my cheeks.

Eyebrows nearly up to her hair, Mama stared at me with her you've-done-it-now look until her mouth twitched into a smile. When she started laughing, I thought I was home free. Mama didn't laugh often, but when she did, anybody in hearing distance had to join in with her trilling yodel. She wouldn't listen when I tried to explain. She just shook her head, saying, "Annie, it's time you learn to be a proper girl."

By the time I washed off most of the mud, a heavy gray stillness had squeezed all the light out of a day that had begun with a sunny sparkle. Rain the night before had washed the world clean and cooled the air. That morning the trees around Dodd's pasture glowed green with freshness against a clear blue sky, and the earth squished soft beneath my feet. James and Robert, my two closest brothers, were picking their way through mucky clay to the pond with Charlie Dodd when James slipped and fell. He grabbed Charlie's leg, and they were both wallowing in the mud.

Charlie scooped up a handful of mud and rubbed it into James's face. They were laughing as hard as Robert and I were. Then Robert dove into the fray. All three of them wrestled and slithered around until they closely resembled the lumps of fudge Mama dropped on wax paper once a year for Christmas.

I was just standing there when that dumb Charlie Dodd grabbed my ankle and pulled me down. "No," I screamed, clutching at tufts of grass that pulled right out of the ground in my hands. My dress slid up, and Charlie rolled over on top of me.

"Leave her alone, Charlie," James said.

But I could take care of myself. I squirmed away from Charlie and kicked my bare foot as hard as I could at his big nose. Then I scrambled out of the mud, and stalked off through waist-high grass in the unused portion of the pasture near the road, leaving a trail of mud splatters.

Charlie had no right to treat me like I was one of the boys. He never would have done that to another girl. Of course, there were no other girls, and I had long held my own with the neighborhood boys. But this time it was different. I wasn't hurt at all, but I was chock full of trembles inside.

Now, Mama was dead serious. She took me by the shoulders and laid down the law. "Annie, you will not go anywhere with the boys again."

"But, Mama."

"No buts." Her piercing blue eyes latched onto mine. "You will stay at home and be a proper girl."

My life was over! No more roaming around the woods looking for bird nests or poking under rocks. No fishing for crawdads in the mud down by the creek or wading over slippery stones in the cool water. No sliding into home just before the ball reached the catcher. What would I do without the boys?

Chapter Two

The next day, I was stuck in the house canning tomatoes with Mama and Miz Lizzie. The kitchen was hotter than a bonfire, and the smothery smell of scalded tomatoes filled the room. I pulled the peel off a steaming tomato and flipped it into the dishpan in my lap. Tomato peel curls were clinging to my wet, wrinkled fingers tighter than a hornworm on a leafless stem.

Outside the kitchen window, the yard shimmered with heat all the way back to the trees bordering the cemetery. Squash leaves in the garden hung limp, withering in the blazing sun. Shouts and whoops of laughter drifted in from the bean patch where James and Robert were supposed to be picking beans. At least they were outside, not trapped in the kitchen, learning to be a lady.

"I'm trying my best to keep George out of the war," Miz Lizzie said. Worms of graying hair had escaped from the bun at her wrinkled neck and crawled toward her face. She pushed a skinned tomato into a jar, mashing it down tight until it was covered with juice. "Now, Edna, you understand," she said. "It's different for you, having five sons. But I have only the one."

Mama sighed, and her lips tightened as she poured boiling water from the teakettle over another pan of

4

tomatoes. Thick steam from the kettle plastered strands of tawny hair to her smooth forehead. "Don't know as it's so different," she muttered before she set the kettle back on the stove.

I knew Mama was thinking about my oldest brother, Richard, joining the army and going off to fight in the Great War. I missed Richard something terrible, and I knew Mama did too. She called him her right-hand man.

When I was little, Richard took care of me if Mama was busy or if she was sick, as she was after the baby was born. Mama was sick a long time after the baby died. I don't remember much about it, but I do know Richard was always there with a hug if I needed one. Richard gave me my doll Ellie that had a china head with a painted face and black painted hair.

Now, Ellie had a cloth face with yarn hair that Aunt Cal gave her after she fell on the floor when James and Robert were playing keep away from me. Richard was the only one to treat me like a girl. He wiped my tears away and held me on his lap after Ellie's head broke. Every night I prayed the war would end so Richard could come home before he got hurt.

I sighed and glanced out the window just in time to see James and then Robert shoot past, headed for the road. "Iceman, iceman, iceman," Paul John chanted as he ran after them as fast as his four-year-old legs could carry him.

The heat of the kitchen and the overwhelming odor of ripe tomatoes were unbearable. "Let me go. Please, Mama." I wiped tomato juice from my hands onto a dishtowel.

"Annie Lou," Mama said. "You're getting too old to run after the iceman every time he comes, like one of the boys."

A cloud of heat settled around my head. Why did I have to stay in the hot kitchen while the boys were outside cooling off with ice? A drop of sweat rolled down my nose and dripped onto the ugly, blood-red pile of tomato peels in my pan.

Mama softened. "Go on this time, but you have to settle down and remember you're a girl."

"I will." My bare feet hardly touched the dry grass as I flew across the yard to the road where two mules pulling the ice wagon came to a halt.

A crowd of boys, including three of my brothers, clustered like a swarm of flies around the iceman. Dan Payne, Aunt Cal's husband, brought ice three times a week in the summer. His dark skin glistened, and his biceps bulged beneath the short sleeves of his blue work shirt as he sawed through a long cake of ice. The boys held their hands under it to catch ice shavings to cram into their mouths and rub over their faces.

"Here, Annie," Robert said as he dumped a few cold slivers into my hands.

The ice melted almost before I got it to my face, but cold water on my cheeks and forehead brought glorious relief from the sweltering heat. I tried to elbow my way through the boys for more ice, but they were pressed so tight around the wagon I could barely get my hand through.

"Here, little lady," Dan Payne said, and a lump of ice dropped into my hand.

I wrapped my fingers around its coldness and said,

"Thank you, Dan," before sliding it into my mouth.

Under the chinaberry tree in the front yard, I sat and watched the boys shoving and scrambling for ice chips. Melting ice trickled down my throat, and a slight breeze lifted my damp curls. Maybe it wasn't so bad being the only girl on Barnes Court.

That afternoon I was washing the dinner dishes when Mama said, "Soon as you finish cleaning up the tomato mess, you can take out a quilt and see if you can get Paul John to rest a while under the trees."

"But, Mama, can't I go down to the creek with the boys? Just this once?"

"Annie, forget the boys." Mama handed me another plate. "Miz Lizzie said Mr. Bolman is bringing the family over for a visit this evening. I know you want to see Rose and Della."

I clattered through those dishes, washing and stacking so fast that Mama said, "Annie. Slow down, girl. You're not going to a fire."

Rose and Della Bolman were my best friends, my only girlfriends, and I had seen them just once since school was out.

The only other girl I'd ever known, not counting the ones I just saw at school, was Elvie Payne, Aunt Cal's daughter. Five years ago, when we turned six, Aunt Cal stopped bringing Elvie when she worked close by. She said Elvie and I both needed friends of our own kind. Elvie probably had lots of colored girlfriends now, but I only had the Bolmans, and they lived so far away I seldom got to see them. I still thought about Elvie a lot.

Later, Paul John was asleep, sandy lashes tight

against his chubby cheeks, almost as soon as he lay down on the quilt under the sugar maple. Trying to keep up with James and Robert wore him out. I waved my hand at a fly that landed on his freckled nose.

Mama said I was lucky to have five brothers, but I longed for a sister. My sister Mary would have been eighteen, one year younger than Richard, if the pneumonia hadn't got her when she was seven. Mama said the Lord gave me to her after Mary was gone, but she still took flowers to Mary's grave in Forest Hill and to the baby's grave, too. The baby came three years after me. She never drew a breath, and she never had a name.

After the baby died, Aunt Cal came over every day for a long time and brought Elvie. Elvie and I were close, like two sides of a dime. When Elvie wasn't there, I cried most of the time. I called the doll Richard gave me Ellie. I couldn't say Elvie.

That's when Mama started letting me do everything James and Robert did.

I lay down next to Paul John and was almost asleep myself when Robert and our towheaded friend, Tommy Pickens, came hustling around the garden. They were bent over with their heads together toting something heavy. A huge watermelon!

"Mr. Eddens give you that?" I called.

"*Shh*," Robert said. "You know that mean man wouldn't give a dog a bone."

Breathing hard, they laid the watermelon on the quilt beside Paul John.

"Remember those two days we worked so hard in the sun, pulling weeds for old man Eddens, and he never gave us a cent," Tommy said. "Well, this is our pay."

"You *stole* a watermelon?" My brothers and I had been in plenty of trouble, leaving Barnett's gate open so the cows got out, accidentally stomping Mrs. Phillanda's prize tulips from Holland, and a few other things. Nobody said we were perfect, but none of us ever stole anything.

"Annie, you were there," Robert said. "You worked as hard as we did. You know Mr. Eddens said he'd pay us. Remember how mad we were when he didn't. Even Daddy was mad about it. This makes us even. One watermelon out of all his won't even be missed."

"We're taking it down to the creek to cool," Tommy said. "The creek's high since it rained, so we can swim a while. Then we'll have a feast."

Juices started running in my mouth just thinking about that cool, sweet watermelon.

Robert grabbed a worn-out, raggedy undershirt of Daddy's that Mama had on the clothesline to wipe it before hanging up the clothes. "We can use this to carry the melon so we don't drop it."

They started off with the watermelon swinging between them, its smooth, green skin showing through the holes in the undershirt.

"Aren't you coming, Annie?" Tommy asked.

"She can't. She's learning to be a girl," Robert said. "I wish you could come, Annie."

"Who said I wanted to come? I'm waiting for Rose and Della." But I did want to go. Rose and Della lived too far away to be part of my everyday life.

Chapter Three

My life was filled with brothers, from Paul John up to Richard. People kept asking if Robert and I were twins. We were about the same size, and you almost never saw one of us without the other. But Robert had his twelfth birthday a month before I turned eleven. James, a year older than Robert and lots bigger, was with the two of us most of the time. William was in high school, and he thought he was grown. Sometimes he worked at one of the cemeteries when they needed extra help, digging graves and tending plants.

My brothers all looked alike, with long legs and big shoulders, and they were covered with freckles the same as I was. We had the same copper-colored hair that darkened as we grew older. Daddy said you could always tell a Davis, but you couldn't tell him much.

The clopping of a horse's hooves and the creak of a wagon on the road brought me to my feet. I ran to the corner of the house and peered at the road. It was the Bolmans, their wagon loaded with baskets of field peas. Mr. Bolman, wearing his flat, leather cap, held the reins while Mrs. Bolman, in her blue sunbonnet, sat tall beside him, making him look even shorter. Rose, Della, and their brother, Herman, waved at me from their seat at the back of the wagon. I waved back and ran toward the house yelling, "They're here! Mama, the

Bolmans are at Miz Lizzie's. Can I go see them?"

"Hush, girl," Mama said. "You know you can't go running over there the minute they come. Give them some time to visit before you go barging in. Sit down now, and help me snap these beans for supper."

I could hardly sit still and snap beans when every inch of me was itching to run outside and across the road to the Adams house. Rose and Della, my best friends in the whole world, were over there visiting their Aunt Lizzie. To satisfy Mama, I managed to keep my fingers busy with the beans until I saw Mr. Bolman lugging a bushel of peas up our back steps. "There's Mr. Bolman!" I hurriedly snapped the last two beans.

"Good to see you, John," Mama said as she crossed the screened porch to open the door. "My goodness, Rose and Della, you girls are almost as tall as your father. Annie, take the girls out under the trees where it's cool."

Before Mama could change her mind, I dashed out the door, grabbed Della's strong, sturdy hand and Rose's little thin one, and raced across the yard. The three of us fell into a laughing heap on the quilt beside the sleeping Paul John. He sat up, rubbed his eyes, and headed toward the house without a word. We laughed harder. Everything was funny when we were together.

"I thought you'd never get here," I said.

"We had to wait till Daddy got home from the cemetery, and we can't stay long." Della brushed her tanned cheek with the bushy end of a fat, sandy-brown braid. "Mother has to get home to milk the cows."

"I have so much to tell you," I said. "Have you heard about the family that's moving into the new house?"

"Over on Hernando?" Rose asked.

"No, that's their business. Daddy told us it's another monument place. He said the family is named Robinson, and they've been very picky about the house," I said. "It's that big one they're building around the corner. They must have a lot of money. And guess what? They have a girl. I can't wait till they move in."

Two pairs of brown eyes gazed into mine. "But you two will still be my best friends," I said.

"Have you seen the new school?" Rose asked.

"Daddy showed it to us after they finished the floors. It has lunchrooms in the basement, one for the boys and one for the girls, and an auditorium upstairs."

"It's much prettier than old Oakland," Della said. "I like the arch over the porch."

"I liked Oakland." Rose traced her finger over some blue briar-stitching on the quilt. "We knew the teachers and all the kids."

Rose was less than a year older than Della and me, but she was much quieter and always had to think things over. Della and I both would do first and think later. Every year Della was the smartest girl in my class, and Robert said the same about Rose. All the girls wanted to be Della's friend.

"Annie." Mama beckoned to us from the back porch.

"Oh, no," Della said. "We have to go."

"Mother said you can come home with us," Rose said. "Ask if you can."

"Girls, your cousin George said you better hurry," Mama called. "Miz Lizzie's waiting supper for you."

"We'll be back," Della yelled as she and Rose ran across the road, tan legs pumping beneath their faded dresses. "Don't forget to ask."

"Ask what?" Mama wanted to know.

"If I can go home with them. Mrs. Bolman said it's all right."

"We'll see."

That's what she always said.

After supper, Robert and I were nearly through washing the mounds of dishes and pots when James opened the screen door for Rose and Della.

"Did you ask?" Della snatched the dishtowel from Robert and dried the last pot while he pestered Rose, holding the ends of her braids like the reins of a horse.

"Mama, you got to let me go," I pleaded. "I never get to go anywhere."

"Well, Annie, I don't know how I can get along without you." Mama swept the last of the supper crumbs into a dustpan.

I couldn't stand it! Della and Rose would be gone in a few minutes, and I wouldn't see them again for no telling how long. I'd have to stay in the house and help Mama. I turned to Daddy who was reading the newspaper at the table. "Daddy?"

He held his pipe in one hand and gave me a slow wink. "Edna, I reckon it won't hurt to let her go. James and Robert can help you in the house for a day or two."

James and Robert groaned at the thought of helping Mama, and I leaped at Daddy and hugged his neck. His auburn beard was soft against my cheek. Then I flung my arms around Mama and squeezed until she gasped, "Mercy, girl, get on out of here."

In the parlor where Paul John and I slept, I opened the tall chifforobe, and Ellie tumbled out, smiling up with her embroidered grin. I quickly stuffed her into a drawer and took out my nightgown and a few other things. Nobody needed to know I still slept with Ellie some nights. "Do I need to bring my shoes? They're too little, and I don't have any new ones yet."

"No," Della said. "You know we don't wear shoes, except on Sunday."

Daylight was beginning to fade as I waved at Mama and Daddy from my seat between Della and Rose at the rear of the Bolmans' wagon. Paul John ran along beside us until he got tired and turned back. I had never stayed a night away from home without some of the family with me, and it seemed strange to see them all standing there while I rode off.

"Can't you make Dolly go a little faster?" Mrs. Bolman asked. "You know the cows are waiting."

Mr. Bolman slapped the reins on the horse's back, and she quickened her pace before slowly returning to a walk. Shadows were getting longer, and leaves whispered in the breeze as Dolly's hooves sent up little puffs of dust from the dirt road.

Empty bushel baskets rocked back and forth beside Herman as he leaned against the side of the wagon. With a big grin, he looked up and said, "Now watch this."

Rose nudged him with her foot. "Oh, Herman. Maybe she won't."

"You know she will. She always does." Herman snickered and pointed at the horse. Dolly daintily stepped into the shallow creek that ran across the road.

When all four of her feet were in the water, she spread her hind legs, and a stream of yellow urine sprayed into the creek.

Herman howled with laughter and rolled about the wagon until Mrs. Bolman said sternly, "Herman, that's enough!"

Holding back a smile, Rose looked sideways at me while Della explained. "Dolly will not cross the creek without stopping to do that. One time we were late to church so Daddy touched her with the whip. She shot off and left Rose, Herman, and me sitting in the dirt with our best clothes on. Since then, we just wait till she's through."

Della's face beamed as she pressed her hand over her mouth. I had a hard time keeping my laugh inside.

Chapter Four

As soon as Dolly pulled the wagon up the hill at the Bolman place and stopped halfway between the house and the barn, Mrs. Bolman slid off the wagon seat. "Girls, take Annie Lou inside and show her where to put her things," she said. "Then you can feed the chickens and gather the eggs. I'm going to get the cows."

I had visited the Bolmans with Mama, but we always left early in the day. The three rooms of the Bolman house were big and almost dark in the scant evening light. A bowl of roses on the kitchen table gave off a faint scent that reminded me of the sweet-smelling toilet water Mama sometimes put behind her ears. In the middle room, a black potbellied stove, waiting for winter, stood between a double bed on one wall and two easy chairs with big, square footstools on the other side of the room. I set my bundle of clothes beside the wardrobe in the front room where Rose and Della slept in a big bed beside the fireplace.

As I followed Rose and Della across the chicken yard, I bent down to scratch a madly itching mosquito bite above my ankle. A huge red rooster with his neck stretched and his head held high stalked toward me. He stopped still, staring me right in the eye. I stood up and he lowered his head, glaring with round black eyes.

Twice his normal size, feathers standing out around his neck, he started scratching the ground like a bull ready to charge. The sharp spurs on his legs looked as long as my finger.

I didn't wait another minute. I ran toward the chicken house just as he hurled himself at me, feet first. My heart beat fast as the rooster hit my leg like a heavy feather duster and slid to the ground. I didn't want Della to know I was afraid of a chicken, so I didn't say anything.

In the musty chicken house, dimly lit by two small windows, Rose picked up a basket and headed toward the nests along the back wall. "I'll get the eggs," she said.

Della filled a bucket with corn from a barrel just inside the door. Three red hens flapped down from the roost to join the others that crowded around Della and me. So many chickens we could hardly walk. As Della tossed corn in wide arcs on the ground, the hens greedily rushed after it. The rooster, with all his attention on the hens, scratched the ground with his yellow feet and picked up kernels in his beak. He made funny chirping noises and shook his long black and red tail-feathers to attract the hens. Most of them paid him no mind as they pecked away at the corn.

"Don't turn your back on Rollo," Della said. "He might jump on you and spur you."

"Thanks for the warning," I said. I was glad Mama had only eleven friendly, white hens and no roosters.

"Mother doesn't like anybody around when she's milking," Della told me. "She says it bothers the cows, but if you're really quiet, we can watch."

In the barn, a caramel-brown cow stood before a feed trough, munching grain while Mrs. Bolman, her flame-colored hair glowing in the light of a nearby lantern, sat on a stool beside the cow. "Now, Brownie, I know I'm late, but I'm here now. You're a good girl," she said. The top of her head brushed the cow's flank as her hands sent streams of milk down into the bucket. Her gentle handling of the cow surprised me. Mrs. Bolman had always seemed so stern and unfeeling that I was never quite comfortable with her.

Four black and white cats and a gray brindled one gathered and sat just inside the barn around an iron skillet with no handle. After milking a second cow, Mrs. Bolman poured the skillet full of milk for the cats. A thin, yellow cat picked her way down the ladder from the loft and added her pink tongue to the others lapping milk.

"Fluff has kittens in the loft. They just got their eyes open a couple of days ago," Rose said. "We'll show you tomorrow."

"Here, Rose, you and Della can carry one of these." Mrs. Bolman set two buckets of milk near us and lifted the lantern.

Rose and Della picked up a bucket between them and slowly walked toward the house, careful not to spill a drop of the creamy white liquid.

Before bedtime, we all gathered in the middle room where, by the light of an oil lamp, Mr. Bolman read aloud a bit from the Bible. Then he read the last two chapters of a book about a mistreated horse called Black Beauty. It took me a while to get used to Mr. Bolman's heavy guttural accent with its strange vowel sounds, but then I was in the story. How could anybody be mean to a horse?

At our house, nobody was ever still long enough to read, and we all went to bed at different times, starting with Paul John, then me, then Robert and on up. Daddy said that was to give Mama a little peace and quiet.

That night as I lay in bed between the Bolman girls, I was wide-awake listening to the night sounds. The clock on the mantel ticked loudly. Rose and Della were asleep, breathing softly. Across the room, Herman flopped about on his half bed making the same boy noises I heard every night at home from my brothers. The chirping of crickets and the ringing buzz of cicadas through open windows sounded much louder than at home.

A floorboard creaked. The back door opened and closed. I sat up, barely breathing, and listened so hard my ears were stiff. Sweat poured down my neck, and I began to shiver. In the heavy darkness, I couldn't see a thing, not even Herman's bed across the room.

"What's the matter?" a sleepy sounding Della whispered.

"I heard something. The door."

"Oh, it's just Daddy. He's always rambling around at night." Della's hand found mine and pulled me out of bed.

"Where're we going?" I whispered.

"Outside. Aren't you hot?"

I stumbled along behind Della, grasping her hand, as we tiptoed through the middle room where soft snoring sounds came from the bed. Della led me through the dark kitchen and outside.

A sliver of a moon and a sky full of stars gave us enough light to see each other, the shapes of trees, and the form of the chicken house. We sat on the steps, breathing in warm night air scented with honeysuckle. Lightning bugs flashed off and on in the darkness.

"I like to come out at night, don't you?" Della said.

"We stay out until after dark playing hide and seek and catching lightning bugs, but when we go in, we have to stay in," I said. "Do you always go to bed so early?"

"Yes, as soon as it gets dark so we don't have to use much coal oil for the lamp. But Daddy goes out almost every night after we're in bed."

"Why does he do that?"

"I don't know," Della said. "I guess he gets hot in the house. You know he came from Switzerland. It's cold over there."

"What does he do outside at night?"

"Whatever he wants, I suppose. He digs in the garden if the moon's bright. Look, there's his lantern over there by the cistern. He's watering the okra."

I could barely make out the shape of Mr. Bolman carrying a sprinkling can. "Doesn't he get tired?"

"Sure he does. Rose, Herman, and I go out at night sometimes, and we've seen Daddy asleep on the ground. Mother said just leave him alone if he wants to sleep outside."

Chapter Five

The next day just after sunup, with our bare feet wet with dew, I helped Rose and Della pick peaches for breakfast and for making preserves.

We washed the breakfast dishes, swept the kitchen floor, fed the chickens, and hurried out to the barn. In the loft we found two gray and two yellow kittens with their mother nestled in a hollow of hay.

"I like this one," Rose said. "He looks like his mama." She picked up one of the yellow ones, a tiny, helpless thing as soft as dandelion fluff, and handed it to me. I held the fat, warm little body up to my cheek, and the kitten began to purr.

"He's yours, if you want him," Della said.

I could not put that kitten down. I named him Dandelion, Dandy for short, and gave him back to Fluff, the mama cat, only for milk. He lay sleeping in my lap that afternoon while Rose and Della helped me make a play skirt like theirs from graveyard ribbons.

After the flowers placed on graves at the cemetery faded, Mr. Bolman brought home beautiful bows of ribbon that had been on wreaths and sprays of flowers. The Bolman garden was bright with ribbons tying up pole beans and tomatoes.

To make my skirt, we untied bows and Rose ironed the ribbons flat. I chose yellow, blue, pink, and red ribbons. Della cut them all the same length, and we started sewing them together long ways.

While I struggled with a red and a yellow ribbon, Rose and Della quickly sewed rows of ribbons together. My thread tangled and knotted constantly. I stuck my fingers with the needle, and my stitches were so big a mouse could have run through the gaps. Rose kept untangling my thread and showing me how to make tiny stitches like hers.

"You know I can't sew," I said. "I hate sewing!"

At my loud voice, Dandy woke up and began mewing. I sweet-talked and petted him, holding him close to my cheek, but he would not stop crying.

"Sewing's not hard, Annie. You can learn." Rose unknotted my thread again.

"Wait, I'm taking Dandy back to Fluff," I said. "He's hungry."

I managed to escape sewing long enough for a quick trip to the barn. Then I really did try to make good stitches, carefully running my needle in and out along the ribbons. I ignored the little stab with each stitch until I reached the end, and I was proud of the shining red and yellow ribbons that lay as one across my lap.

"Look what you've done," Rose said. "It looks great. Give it to me, and I'll stitch it to mine and Della's. We have enough for your skirt."

Rose reached for my sewing and pulled, but it went nowhere. She and Della began laughing as I sat there with a dumb grin. I had stitched the ribbons to my dress.

I never did want to sew. Mama had been trying to

teach me for the past year, but I had better things to do than sit around poking my fingers with a needle. I didn't want to cook either. In fact, I was just like my brothers. I didn't want to do any housework.

Finally, with all of us working together, me holding the ribbons mostly, we finished my skirt and I put it on. It was beautiful, ankle length with gathers at the waist and bright ribbon stripes around it.

Rose and Della made ribbon dresses for their dolls, and Herman wrapped a red ribbon around Silly Dilly, a gray cat that didn't seem to mind what anybody did to him. "If you're dressed up, Silly Dilly," Herman said, "you have to wear shoes." He tied pieces of newspaper around the cat's feet with string. When he set him down, Silly Dilly shook one foot and then another in a funny dance of hops and kicks.

We all laughed until our sides hurt. Then softhearted Rose reached for the cat and pulled off his dancing shoes. "You don't like those old shoes, do you, boy?" She took off the ribbon and smoothed Silly Dilly's fur until he calmed down.

Then the girls had to peel peaches and help Mrs. Bolman make preserves. We talked and laughed while we worked. It was fun to see who could get the longest curl of peel before it broke.

That evening we gathered in the middle room with Mr. and Mrs. Bolman in their big easy chairs. Mr. Bolman said, "Look in my bag and see what I got at the library."

Della and Herman rushed to the white feed sack Mr. Bolman always carried with him. I had often wondered what he had in that bag. Tonight it was lumpy and full to the top.

"Be careful with the bread," Mrs. Bolman said.

Della opened the bag and pulled out two loaves of rye bread and one of whole wheat. She handed them to Rose and me to put in the kitchen breadbox. That bread smelled so good I wanted to tear into it though I was still stuffed from all the vegetables, cornbread, and peach cobbler I ate for supper.

Next out of the bag were three books from the library. Della's face lit up as she held one high. "Look, it's *Little Women*!"

"Good, that's the one I've been wanting to hear," Mrs. Bolman said. "Now put away the rest of that stuff."

Herman took two empty fruit jars to the kitchen while Della gathered up seed packets, a file, three little clay pots, and two pink ribbon bows to put in a box by the back door.

"Rose," Mr. Bolman said, "put my newspaper back in the bag and hand me my bank book before it gets lost. I've saved up nearly enough for another Liberty Bond."

Rose picked up a newspaper covered with the strangest print. I couldn't read a word of it. "What kind of paper is that?"

"That's Daddy's Swiss newspaper," Rose said. "It's in German. He always gets one when he goes downtown to the bakery."

"He can read German?" I didn't know anybody who knew a language other than English. I should have guessed Mr. Bolman did, though. He had such a heavy accent.

"Of course," Rose said. "That's what he spoke in Switzerland."

The next morning I sat on the wagon seat beside Mr. Bolman. He was taking me home on his way to work at the Jewish cemetery. I felt I should say something to him, but I didn't know what. When I gave him a half smile, he seemed to be concentrating on a spot between Dolly's ears. "I had a lovely time with Rose and Della," I finally said.

"Good, that's good," Mr. Bolman said with a nod. "You come any time." He never had much to say.

Rose told me he reads to them at night because Mrs. Bolman can't see well enough to read. She can't sew either because of her eyes, so Rose and Della do all the mending. I didn't know Mrs. Bolman was partially blind. Maybe that's why she seems so stern, always frowning and staring. Della said she went to a school for the blind when she was young, and she learned to see better than she could before.

Rose and Della worked as much or more than I did at home, but there were two of them, and it was fun working with them. I wouldn't mind doing housework with another girl. Girls at school were always talking about staying the night at one house or another, but I was never invited. Maybe when the new girl moved in, we would be friends and could help each other with our chores.

Dandy was the sweetest little kitten. How was I going to tell Mama about him? She didn't take much to pets. She thought everything should earn its keep. I could tell her Dandy would grow up to be a fine mouser like Miz Lizzie's black cat, Elvira. Before Dandy was old enough to leave the mama cat, I had to convince Mama to let me keep him.

As Mr. Bolman turned Dolly off Hernando and onto Barnes Court, Paul John charged out of the house. "The new girl was here," he yelled, "wearing shoes and everything. You should see her. She's pretty."

Mama nodded from the porch and said, "Mrs. Robinson and Iris Elizabeth were here yesterday. They were disappointed that you weren't around."

Iris Elizabeth. What a beautiful name!

Chapter Six

"They're moving in. Come on, Annie." Robert gulped the last of his water and turned to leave. "Don't you want to watch?"

"Mama?" I folded another towel and laid it on the stack of clean ones. We had washed clothes all morning and took them off the line right after dinner. A pile of clothes still on the bed waited to be folded.

"You can go for a little while, Annie," Mama said. "But all of you stay back out of the way. You hear?"

Robert, Paul John, and I joined a group of boys at the side of the road. "Where're they going to put all that stuff?" Robert asked as we watched men unload furniture from two huge motor vans.

"That's a big house, upstairs and down," I said, hoping to catch a glimpse of Iris Elizabeth.

"I don't know why they're starting another monument place right next to the old one," James said to Charlie Dodd.

"Mr. Robinson told my pop he'd never seen a better location, across the road from three cemeteries. He said he'd make a killing," Charlie said.

"Look, they have a piano!" Paul John pointed at four husky men struggling up the six broad steps of the new house with a baby grand.

"*Annieee*," Mama's voice rang out, calling me

home. "*Annieee*," she called again, louder than before.

I didn't dare ignore that call if I ever expected to go anywhere again. "You tell me everything you see," I told Robert before I ran across the road toward Mama.

At the supper table, a steady stream of talk about the new neighbors accompanied the clatter and scrape of knives and forks.

"And that's when the family drove up in a royal blue, four-season sedan," Robert said as he reached for another piece of cornbread.

"They have a car?" William looked down the table at Daddy. "Maybe they'll let me drive it." William was crazy about automobiles.

"Why would they?" James said. "It's a new car. I saw it. Besides, they don't even know you."

Daddy pushed himself back from the table and took out his pipe. "Well, I reckon we've talked enough about the new neighbors. You know all about them, and they're just moving in."

"I don't know much, Daddy," I said. "I don't even know how many kids they have."

"Far as I know, there's just the girl," Daddy said. "And the two of them."

"Why do they need such a big house?" Paul John asked.

"Sometimes, it's not so much what you need," Mama said, "as what you want."

The next morning I was clearing the breakfast table when Mama said, "Get that basket of peaches Mr. Bolman left. It's enough for two cobblers, one for us and one for the Robinsons."

"And we can take it over there so I can meet Iris

Elizabeth." I loved the way that name rolled off my tongue. Last night, after the house was quiet, I lay in bed thinking about Iris Elizabeth, wondering if a rich girl would like me.

I washed the peaches and began to peel before Mama had time to dump the dishwater on the petunias beside the back steps.

That afternoon, after Mama warned Robert not to leave Paul John by himself, we started down the road to the Robinson house. The mouth-watering smell of the peach cobbler Mama carried escaped from its wax paper covering, and I could almost taste its sweet goodness.

We climbed wide steps to the heavy oak door, and Mama knocked. A snow-white calla lily bloomed in the blues and greens of the door's stained glass window. My throat ached with the beauty of it. We waited and waited.

"Maybe they're not home," Mama said.

As we turned to leave, the door opened a crack, and a cold voice announced, "The Robinsons do not respond to solicitations."

She thought we wanted money, or to sell something! We were trying to be friendly, and we were as welcome as a couple of stray cats. I wanted to scuttle into the tall grass across the road and hide like a field mouse.

In a thin, strained voice, Mama explained. "We brought over a fresh peach cobbler for you, Mrs. Robinson, just to be neighborly."

The door opened barely wide enough for a hand to reach out and take the cobbler. "That's nice of you,

Mrs. Davis, but we're not accepting callers at this time."

"Mother, is it Annie?" came a voice from behind the door.

"Be quiet, sweetie," the woman said as she peered out at us with eyes so green they reminded me of a grass snake. Her smooth, black hair framed a round, pasty-white face. "Do you know where I can get some household help?" she said. "I've never been without help."

Mama looked off down the road a while before she answered. "Aunt Cal helps the Bolmans around the place and takes in ironing. You might get her or Aunt Loma. They've both helped me with the babies."

"Are they Negroes?" Mrs. Robinson asked.

"Yes, and they are both good workers," Mama said.

"I don't know." Mrs. Robinson raised her thin eyebrows. "But I do need help, and I could keep a close eye on them." She pulled the door shut without another word.

"Somebody needs to keep an eye on her," Mama muttered. "Let's go home, Annie." She stalked home with a grim look on her face. Mama's mouth had never been so tightly closed and turned down at the corners.

Big as I was, I wanted to cry. I was counting on getting to know Iris Elizabeth. Now Mama had her feelings hurt, and I didn't know what to think about the new girl.

Chapter Seven

A week later, I was helping Paul John wash some rocks he claimed were special treasures when Aunt Cal came lumbering across the yard. "Mama, Aunt Cal's here," I called.

Mama pushed open the screen door with a dishpan of peas she was shelling. "Aunt Cal, come and sit a while," she said. She sat on the top step and patted a spot beside her. "It's too hot for you to be out walking in this heat. Let me get you some water."

"No, ma'am. Don't trouble yourself none." With the hem of her big, white apron, Aunt Cal wiped beads of sweat off her glistening, brown forehead and dropped her weight on the step. "I just come from over to the Robinsons. Mrs. Robinson told me to give you this." She handed Mama a small white envelope.

"Is she treating you all right?" Mama gave Aunt Cal a long look. "I started not to give her your name, or Aunt Loma's."

"Honey, don't you worry about ole Cal. She's paying me, and I don't give her no mind, knowing she's from the north."

My eyes were glued to Mama's hands as she ran her finger along the seal of the envelope and pulled out the message. "Annie," she said slowly, "Mrs. Robinson's inviting us to call tomorrow afternoon. You think we should go?"

Go? More than anything I wanted to meet Iris Elizabeth and have a girlfriend in the neighborhood. But I remembered the look on Mama's face after Mrs. Robinson closed her door. I remembered picking peaches in McKenzie's orchard later, feeling as rotten as the overripe fruit on the ground. "You decide, Mama," I said.

Mama gazed at the little card covered with spidery script. Then she stuck it back in the envelope and turned to Aunt Cal. "Tell her we'll be there."

Around Barnes Court, being at a neighbor's house was just like being at home. Visitors pitched in and helped with whatever chores needed to be done, knowing the favor would be returned later. Nobody ever dressed up to visit a neighbor. But the next day, Mama and I dolled ourselves up in our church clothes before going over to the Robinsons' house.

Mama did look pretty in her best dress. Hot as it was, she had put on stockings and was wearing her wide-brimmed hat with a blue bow to match her dress. I had on the dress I wore for Easter, a little faded but freshly starched and ironed. It had belonged to Charlie Dodd's older sister, Susan, the one who ran off with the man who came around selling dried herbs and spices. The thing I hated was squeezing my feet into my tight shoes just to go around the corner, but I did it.

This time the oak door opened wide, and Aunt Cal said, "Mrs. Mary Robinson and Miss Iris Elizabeth await your company in the parlor." That didn't sound like Aunt Cal at all.

As she led us to the parlor, I peered around Aunt

Cal's broad back to see Iris Elizabeth sitting properly in a ruby red, velvet chair, her hands in her lap and her ankles crossed. From the pink bow holding back her dark curls to the tips of her shiny black shoes, she was perfect, so pretty, like a china doll. Her green eyes stared into mine until her mother said, "Speak up, Iris Elizabeth. Remember your manners."

She got up from her velvet chair and offered her hand to Mama and said, "Good afternoon, Mrs. Davis. I am so glad you could come." Then she turned to me. "You must be Annie."

I took her soft, white hand in my freckled, tan one and managed to stammer, "Pleased to meet you." My face was red hot as I compared her smooth, oval fingernails to my ragged ones lined with hangnails.

"Have a seat, Mrs. Davis and Annie," Mrs. Robinson said in a honeyed voice as she waved toward the end of the sofa she sat on and another velvet chair. "Bring in the tray now, Cal. We'll have some lemonade and cookies."

Watching Iris Elizabeth, I spread my napkin over my lap as she did. She cocked her head and listened to the adults as she daintily nibbled cookies and sipped lemonade. Struggling to keep my napkin in place and my crumbs on the napkin, I drank most of the icy, sweet drink before I lowered the glass to see Iris Elizabeth looking at me. As those enchanting eyes gazed into mine, I was thrilled to think that this girl could possibly be my friend.

"We've never lived in such a rural area before," Mrs. Robinson said. "I'm afraid the culture here is very different from what we've previously known. I do hope

Iris Elizabeth will be able to continue her piano lessons. She loves music and plays quite nicely, you know."

"I'm sure you can find a music teacher here if you want one," Mama said. "Even in Memphis we have schools, churches, and theaters, all with pianos and people who play them."

The talk went on and on until Mrs. Robinson remembered us and said, "You girls may go upstairs now. Iris Elizabeth, show Annie your room and your dresses and things."

"Yes, Mother." Iris Elizabeth primly nodded to me, and I followed her up the curved staircase, sliding my hand along the smooth top of the ornately carved banister. I felt as out of place as a hound dog in a hospital.

"Whew! Am I glad to get out of there," Iris Elizabeth whispered as she pulled me into a fairy tale room with rosebud wallpaper and a canopy bed covered with pink flounces and ruffles. "Now we can have some fun."

"I thought you were having fun downstairs."

"You don't mean it! That's just part of the game." Iris Elizabeth scooped up five gorgeous dolls from a settee and carelessly dumped them on the bed.

"Oh, be careful," I said. "You don't want to break them. They're beautiful."

"You like dolls?" Her eyebrows flew up, and I wondered if I should like dolls. "You can have any one you want if we get to be friends," she said. "Do you know any boys?"

"That's all I do know. I have five brothers and there are plenty more boys around here. I was the only girl until you came."

"Not really! What is your school like?"

"We have a brand new school, Ford N. Taylor, just past the cemeteries and around the corner on Alice Avenue," I said. "It'll have grades one to eight."

"Boys and girls?"

After I nodded, she burst out, "I've never gone to a public school. I've always been in a private girls' school. Mother wanted me to go to St. Agnes Academy here, but I convinced Father I needed to broaden my experiences to really be educated. As if I wanted to be educated. So I'll be going to school with you."

"Come, see my clothes." She threw open the doors of an oversized wardrobe. "Here are my new dresses, and these are my old ones. Mother bought my new clothes in Cincinnati because she was afraid Memphis wouldn't have a good selection of quality clothing to choose from."

The wardrobe was overflowing with dresses of all styles and colors, but I didn't see any old dresses. I did see five pairs of shoes and a blue coat with a fur collar and cuffs.

"And these drawers have my socks and ribbons to match the dresses. You don't talk much, do you, Annie?"

How could I squeeze in a word with her chattering? Even if I had something to say.

"Miss Iris Elizabeth," Aunt Cal called up the stairs. "Mrs. Mary Robinson wants you and Miss Annie to come down right now."

Aunt Cal had never called me Miss Annie before, and I didn't like it. When I was little, she would hold

Elvie and me on her big, soft lap as she sang and rocked us after dinner. Aunt Cal was almost like a mother to me. She shouldn't be calling me Miss Annie.

Chapter Eight

I tickled Dandy under the chin and let him climb up my dress to nuzzle my neck. When Mr. Bolman drove up early this morning, saying he brought my cat, I was afraid Mama would have a fit. I hadn't told her about Dandy. I just knew she wouldn't let me keep him, but she did. Maybe because I can't play with the boys any more. It's all right for girls to have cats. "Mama, look at him. Isn't he sweet? He's the softest thing."

"Girl, give that cat some milk and put it outside so we can get some work done around here," Mama said. "You haven't done a lick of work since Mr. Bolman brought the cat."

I filled a saucer with milk and left Dandy drinking beside the petunias with Paul John to watch him. Then I finished up the dishes and sprinkled down the starched clothes. I loved the clean smell of the starch and the way the stiff, wrinkled shirts and dresses wilted when water from the sprinkling bottle hit. I rolled the damp clothes and packed them in a basket for Mama to iron. She said I had to watch because I'd be doing that job soon.

Girls, except for Iris Elizabeth, had entirely too much work to do. I had visited her a number of times since the day I went to her house with Mama, but I'd never seen Iris Elizabeth do a bit of work.

That girl loved to talk. She was better than a storybook. A couple of days ago, she told me about her neighbor Lily in Cincinnati. She said, "Lily was stepping out with a fine young man that her parents wanted her to marry, but I knew she'd never marry him."

"How did you know?"

"I just knew. He was too bookish and not nearly as handsome as her other beau. Most nights after her parents were asleep, Lily would leave with her real love, walk down the street with him to the corner and then ride off on his motorcycle with him. I'd see them from my window. Isn't that the most romantic thing you ever heard?"

Iris Elizabeth leaned toward me and whispered, "I know a lot of things."

"What kind of things?" I'd never heard such talk before.

"A new girl, Lenora Hamilton, came to our school. She had long blond curls. The girls in our class thought she was wonderful, but I knew that wouldn't last."

"You did?"

Iris Elizabeth raised her eyebrows and gave me a nod. "Lenora stole the teacher's Moroccan leather pencil box. She said she didn't, but they found it in her desk. After that, none of the other girls would talk to her. She was so miserable her parents put her in another school."

"Now you tell me something." Iris Elizabeth leaned back on her settee, folded her arms, and waited.

I couldn't tell her anything. I didn't know anything. She would think I was as dull as dishwater. After a long silence, I said, "I know a man who goes out at night."

"That's nothing. Lots of men go out at night."

"But he stays outside and sleeps on the ground some nights."

"Now that's strange." Iris Elizabeth's eyes widened. "Who is it?"

"Mr. Bolman. He works at the Jewish cemetery."

"Now that's funny." She giggled and poured herself another glass of lemonade. "Maybe a Jewish ghost has him under a spell."

I shouldn't have told her that. I didn't like her laughing about Mr. Bolman.

Iris Elizabeth was a puzzle to me. One minute she was chatty and confiding like the friend I'd hoped for. Then she was a boasting show-off. When we were in the parlor under her mother's eye, listening to music on the Victrola, Iris Elizabeth was as proper as a girl could be. But when we were up in her room with her store-bought paper dolls, she said all kinds of outlandish things. Maybe girls did talk about grownup subjects, but Rose and Della and I never did. Even Mama and Mrs. Bolman never said right out the word that meant going to have a baby.

Iris Elizabeth had probably never washed a dish in her life, and she had no idea what it was like to run barefoot down a hill or play crack the whip with a bunch of boys. I'd never known anybody like her.

After Mama said I couldn't go to the Robinsons' house again until Iris Elizabeth came to ours, Mrs. Robinson finally said she could come today. On a quilt under the maple tree, Iris Elizabeth sat with her legs tucked under her skirt, barely showing the tips of her shiny shoes. In her ruffled dress, she looked as uncomfortable as I felt in her house with its fine carpets and Queen Anne furniture. Those chairs and tables with their curved legs looked like they might take off running any second, like that old white bulldog of Mr. Adams.

As Dandy lay sleeping, Iris Elizabeth ran one finger down his back from his head to his tail. "Where'd you get the kitten?"

"Mr. Bolman brought him to me this morning. Isn't he cute?"

"Mr. Bolman! That funny little man who works at the Jewish cemetery? Daddy pointed him out to me. Why would he bring you a cat?"

"His daughters, Rose and Della, are my best friends. They gave Dandy to me."

Iris Elizabeth folded her arms and glared at me. "I thought I was your best friend."

"You are, but Rose and Della are my other best friends."

"You can't have but one best friend, Annie. You know my doll you like, the one with the golden curls and the pink dress. I was planning to give you that one, but now I don't know."

No matter what Iris Elizabeth said, I would never give up Rose and Della. "Maybe we could all be best friends."

Iris Elizabeth picked at a ruffle on her dress and said, "Mother wouldn't want me to be friends with a gravedigger's daughters. Your father being a carpenter is not quite so bad."

I looked at Iris Elizabeth, and I could see Mrs. Robinson's green eyes as she closed the door on Mama. I bent over Dandy and touched the soft hair behind his ears.

"Now don't get mad." Light as a butterfly's touch, Iris Elizabeth's hand rested for a moment on my arm. "Let's be friends." She pulled a small tin box out of her pocket. "Here, have some chocolates."

The sweet chocolate melted on my tongue, and I couldn't help smiling. At our house we never saw chocolate except at Christmas or some other special occasion. Iris Elizabeth wanted to be my friend.

"Mail!" Robert called as he ran around the corner of the house toward the back door. "We got the new Sears and Roebuck catalog."

Chapter Nine

"Let's go see if we got a letter from Richard." I pulled Iris Elizabeth to her feet.

"Who's Richard?"

"My oldest brother. He's over in France in the war," I called back to her as I raced across the yard. "We haven't heard from him in a long time."

Mama gave a weak smile and tucked a strand of hair behind her ear. "No, Annie, there is no letter today. Now take Iris Elizabeth back outside where it's cool."

"Your mother is not well, is she?" Iris Elizabeth said as we settled ourselves on the quilt again. "She is so thin."

"She's not sick. She's just worried about Richard."

"Well, I think she needs to plump up. She would be so much more attractive if she wasn't so skinny."

"Mama is too busy to worry about being attractive," I said. "Besides, I like her the way she is." Mrs. Robinson never did anything but give orders to Aunt Cal and sit around eating. No wonder she had plenty of meat on her bones.

"You don't have to get huffy," Iris Elizabeth said. "I was just trying to help."

"You worry too much about looks. Here you are in those socks and shoes and a pettislip, and I'll bet you're burning up in this heat. You can't run or do anything in shoes like that."

"Why would I want to run? Annie, you've been around too many boys. Girls don't run."

"I do, and Rose and Della do, too."

"Barefoot?" Iris Elizabeth looked at my feet as if she'd never seen anything so ugly. "You run barefoot with the boys?"

I stood up, conscious that the feet I'd washed last night before bedtime were no longer clean. They were positively grubby, covered with dust, a line of dirt under several toenails. "Yes, we run barefoot," I almost shouted. "It's fun. You should stay over here at night. We play hide and seek when it starts to get dark, and all of us are barefoot."

That evening at our supper table, Iris Elizabeth looked from one Davis to another, watching huge amounts of food disappear as bowls and platters passed around the table, accompanied by loud laughing and talking.

"Anybody with a brain would rather have a motorcycle," James said. "You can ride it on or off the road."

"Only one, or maybe two, can ride a motorcycle," William said. "I'll take a car any time."

"Not me," James said, shaking his head. "I'm saving up for an Indian."

"And some stormy day I'll see you looking like a drowned rat while I'm nice and dry in my four-season." William laughed and elbowed Iris Elizabeth sitting next to him. "Right, Iris?"

When she gave a quick nod and looked down at her

plate, I felt a quirk of satisfaction. All her social graces had not prepared Iris Elizabeth to deal with the Davis boys.

"I would like to buy an Indian," Paul John said as his fork chased peas into his mashed potatoes. "He could teach me how to shoot a bow and arrow."

The kitchen exploded with snorts and guffaws that went on until Mama said, "Excuse us, Iris Elizabeth. Some of us seem to have forgotten our manners." She glared at Robert who was still snickering between bites.

Daddy patted Paul John's shoulder and said, "Don't worry about it, little man. An Indian is a kind of motorcycle."

When I ate with the Robinsons, I worried the whole time about using the wrong fork, or picking up the wrong glass. And the silence was broken only by an occasional comment from Mr. or Mrs. Robinson. It seemed that we were on stage, and nothing was real. A tremendous amount of food was left in the bowls that Aunt Cal carried away when we were through. I wondered what happened to it. I couldn't see the Robinsons eating leftovers.

Most nights after supper, when the neighbors came over, the grownups sat on the front porch talking while the boys and I played games, but tonight I sat with Iris Elizabeth on the steps, listening to the adults.

Mr. Robinson came to get Iris Elizabeth, and he leaned against the wall, smoking a sweet-smelling cigar. "Well, I say the only good Hun is a dead Hun, and I'm talking about the ones in this country, too," he said. "You know the trouble they had last week at the foundry works with the niggers wanting more money.

It was the Germans that stirred them up."

"Oh, I don't know," Daddy said. "They were only making four bucks a day. The Germans have been pretty good for Memphis, and generous with their pocketbooks, too. In particular, before the yellow fever."

"That's ancient history, Davis," Mr. Robinson said. "I'm talking about the present. I guess you didn't hear about the trouble in town today."

"No, I guess I didn't," Daddy said.

"Listen to this. About thirty girls had been hired by the U. S. Employment Service to work at the gunpowder plant in Nashville. They'd make a little cash and serve the country, too," Mr. Robinson said. "Well, they were just boarding the train for Nashville, when some German propagandist spread the word that they'd be held in bondage for six months, not even allowed to talk or write to family and friends."

"You don't say," Mama said.

"Sure did." Mr. Robinson went on. "Scared those girls to death. They rushed off that train and out of Union Station. Some of them even left their baggage. A Hun lie! That's what it was, a Hun lie."

"You're saying we have Germans here in Memphis who support the German war effort?" Daddy asked.

"I am, and not so far away," Mr. Robinson said. "I'd keep my eye on your friend, John Bolman, if I were you. He was in town today. I saw him getting off the streetcar myself."

"That's enough," Mama said firmly. "Annie, tell Iris Elizabeth good night. It's time for you to go in."

Mama never let me hear anything important. I

wanted to slap that pleased look off Iris Elizabeth's face. Rose and Della's father had nothing to do with any Huns. Before I could hear anything else, Mama hauled me off into the house.

Chapter Ten

The next morning when I came into the kitchen, Mama was wearing one of her two best dresses covered by her usual apron. "Where're you going?" I asked as I tried to get the tangles out of my wild hair.

"Did you forget? This is the day we shop for school clothes. Hurry and get your hair combed and put on your shoes. The Bolmans will be here right after breakfast. Mr. Bolman's bringing them over on his way to work." Mama slapped a dollop of scrambled eggs on each plate for Robert to put on the table.

"Breakfast," she called. "Come and get it while it's hot." She pulled a pan of biscuits from the oven to serve with a bowl of milk gravy and a plate of bacon.

I had been waiting the whole summer for shopping day, but lately I had been so busy with Iris Elizabeth I forgot today was the day. Every morning, I hurried through my chores so I could spend the rest of the day with her. After trying so hard to be the kind of girl Iris Elizabeth would like, I was ready for a day with Rose and Della. They knew the real me.

The talk about Mr. Bolman and the Huns had stayed with me all night. Sitting between Rose and Della on the streetcar that went from the turn-around at Forest Hill Cemetery to Main Street, I hoped they would never know that some people thought their father was helping the Germans.

Mama and Mrs. Bolman sat in the seat ahead of us, talking over Paul John's head.

"Have to pick out a few things for the boys and just hope they fit," Mama said. "Won't need to get much. Harriette, you know with five boys we have plenty of hand-me-downs."

"My sister gave me clothes her children outgrew for the girls and Herman," Mrs. Bolman said. "Thank the Lord for that. These children are growing like weeds."

I exchanged smiles with Rose and Della. "I met the new girl," I said. "Iris Elizabeth's her name, and you should see her house. She has a room of her own, pink with rosebud wallpaper and five china dolls all lined up on a settee. She said she'd give me one."

"What's she like? Iris Elizabeth?" Rose asked.

"It's hard to say. She never plays with boys, but she talks about them all the time. Her mother thinks she loves to play the piano, but she hates it. She always wears Sunday clothes, and she'll be in seventh grade like you, Rose." I stopped. I didn't want to talk about Iris Elizabeth any more.

Leaving the mothers to plod along with Paul John, I skipped with Rose and Della from the car stop to Goldsmith's Department Store on Main Street. Just inside the entrance was a huge barrel decorated with red, white, and blue ribbons and labeled *Liberty Peach Stones*. A sign said fruit pits and nut shells of every kind were needed to make gas masks to protect U. S. soldiers in chemical warfare.

"Look!" Della said. "They can make gas masks out

of seeds."

I read the sign again. "I'll start collecting seeds as soon as I get home." Richard was in that war, and if he needed a gas mask, I would do everything I could to get him one.

"There are a lot of peach, plum, and apricot seeds on the ground under the trees at home," Della said. "We can gather them, and Daddy can bring them down here for us."

"I think everybody should do all they can for the war effort," Rose said. "Daddy bought a Liberty Bond, and he's saving for another one."

"Annie, did you know Cousin George joined the army?" Della asked. "Aunt Lizzie tried to keep him from going. But he said he was grown and she couldn't stop him."

"William wants to go, but Mama won't let him," I said. "She thinks one son over there is enough for her."

Mama held the heavy, glass door open for Mrs. Bolman and Paul John. "You are so right. Besides, William is too young to be going to war, even if he has done a man's job at the cemetery with Mr. Bolman this summer."

"John says William's a good gravedigger, cuts the sides straight down," Mrs. Bolman said. "He's going to miss William when he starts back to school."

In the girls' department Rose, Della, and I chose identical gingham dresses with white collars for the first day of school, red for Rose, blue for Della, and green for me.

In the shoe store I showed Mama some pretty shoes like the ones Iris Elizabeth wore, but she bought me some sturdy, brown oxfords. She said pretty little shoes like Iris Elizabeth's wouldn't last long. I wore the new shoes and carried the old ones in the store bag. With all the walking from store to store up and down Main Street looking for bargains, those new shoes rubbed blisters on my feet until they hurt worse than the old ones did.

At noon Mama and Mrs. Bolman spread an old sheet on the grass near the fountain in Court Square, and we all sat down to eat the sandwiches we brought from home. The coos of pigeons begging crumbs from picnickers in the square mingled with the splish-splash of the fountain. Water spouted into the air and sparkled in the sunlight as it dropped into one basin, and then another, before splashing into the pool around the fountain.

"Mama, I want in the water." Paul John laid down his half-eaten ham sandwich.

To my surprise, Mama slipped off his shoes and socks so he could play in the pool with two little boys pouring water on their heads with a couple of tin cans.

A squirrel that looked as soft as Dandy sat a few feet away, staring at me. I'd been worried about leaving Dandy for so long, but I'd asked Robert to watch him while I was gone. I tore off a bit of bread and tossed it to the squirrel. He grabbed it and ran behind a tree.

"There's another one." Della pointed. "And another."

We fed crumbs to the squirrels while pigeons flocked around to snatch what they could.

"Listen," Rose said. "Music."

The sound of an accordion attracted a crowd of

children to the far side of the square. They followed a man with a tiny American flag stuck in his hatband as he marched up to the bandstand near the fountain. He stopped there and played patriotic songs on his accordion. "Over there, over there, the Yanks are coming," he sang.

Mrs. Bolman and another lady started singing. Mama and the rest of us joined in. Soon most all the people there were singing, "Long may our land be bright, with freedom's holy light..."

Mr. Robinson had to be wrong when he said some people in Memphis were for the Germans. Certainly Mr. Bolman was not!

Sweat trickled down my back, and my feet burned inside the stiff, new shoes. I untied and loosened the laces, wishing I could cool off in the water like Paul John.

"You girls could put your feet in the pool," Mrs. Bolman suggested, as if she could read my mind.

Sore spots on my feet showed red and raw through the clear water, but they felt much better. I'd have to wear my new shoes a little every day until I got used to them. Maybe by the time school started, I'd be able to stand them all day.

An arc of water shot through the air from Della's direction and hit Paul John in the back. When he looked around, Della was innocently rippling the water with her hand.

"Show me," I said as she shot another squirt, hitting one of the other little boys on the shoulder.

Della showed me how to launch an arc of water from my clasped hands, and we shot the little boys every time Mrs. Bolman and Mama looked away. I knew Mama would tell us to act our age and be ladies if she saw us. We were giggling at our latest hits when one of the boys ran at me with a can of water and dumped it on my head.

"That's it," Mama said. "Time to go. Get dried off." She reached for Paul John. "Boy, you are soaking wet, pants and all. Run around in the sun and dry yourself before we get on the streetcar." She never said a word to me, but I think she and Mrs. Bolman saw all our fun.

Della dried her feet on a big man's handkerchief Mrs. Bolman handed her and then gave it to me. I got most of the water off my head and feet and stuffed my poor feet into my old shoes that didn't feel much better than the new ones.

"We'll always be best friends, won't we?" Della said.

"Just like the three musketeers," Rose said.

"Who are the three musketeers?" I asked.

"They're three best friends in a book Daddy's reading to us," Della said. "They were men who served the king and their country with their swords."

"We can serve our country by collecting seeds and nuts for gas masks," I said.

"We could be the three musketeers," Rose said. "And Iris Elizabeth could be D'Artagnan. D'Artagnan was the real good friend of the three musketeers."

Iris Elizabeth would like Rose and Della. How could she not?

Loaded with packages, we all squeezed onto the crowded streetcar and headed for home when the stores began to close that afternoon. Pressed between Mama and a man I didn't know, I clutched a pole and swayed with the other people as the streetcar stopped and started. By the time we were halfway to the end of the line, the crowd had thinned out, and we all had a seat.

Sucking on horehound candy, I sat between Rose and Della, wishing the day didn't have to end. At the same time, I wondered what Iris Elizabeth would have thought of our fun in the park.

Chapter Eleven

In the dark my heart pounded as I raced through giant trees. Underbrush grabbed at my legs. I looked and looked for Richard. I had to give him a gas mask and tell him the Germans were coming with chemicals. A great boom shook the earth, and I fell trembling to the ground. Bullets whizzed overhead, and I hugged the damp earth, straining to see through a cloud of fog.

"Wake up, Annie. You're dreaming. Wake up, honey." Mama's voice broke through my nightmare, and I woke sobbing and clinging to my pillow.

"Oh, Mama, I wanted to help Richard, but I couldn't find him." The horror of the dream was still with me. I would never forget it.

"Annie, I don't want you listening to the men talk about the war any more," Mama said as she rubbed my back.

Paul John was patting my arm and staring at me with wide eyes.

"I'm fine now." I hated to be such a bother. "You can go back to bed, Mama. I'll read to Paul John so he can get to sleep again."

Paul John finally dozed off after three stories from the big, red fairy tale book. I quietly got up from his cot, turned off the light, and went back to my bed on the sofa.

I could not stop thinking about Richard. After he joined the army, a letter with a special note for me came from him almost every day. Now it had been weeks since his last letter. The day he arrived in France, he wrote that his company was excited about fighting. They didn't think it would take long to beat the Huns and push them all the way back to Germany.

I stared into the darkness a long time. War was a terrible thing.

The next afternoon I was wearing the ribbon skirt I made with Rose and Della when Iris Elizabeth found Dandy and me on the quilt under the maple tree.

"What a great play skirt!" she said. "You could be a princess at the ball or a debutante going out with her beau in that. Where did you get it?"

"I made it. Rose and Della both have one. We made them out of graveyard ribbons Mr. Bolman brought home."

"You shouldn't be so friendly with the Bolmans," Iris Elizabeth said. "You can't trust any Germans. My father said nobody knows what Mr. Bolman carries in that white bag of his."

"I know what he has in it, just bread and books and regular stuff. He wouldn't hurt anybody. Besides he's not even German. He came from Switzerland, just like his aunt, Miz Lizzie Adams."

"Well, he sounds like a German. So does Miz Lizzie. But her husband, Mr. Adams, is a plain American. And their son George joined the army. With a name like Adams, a person couldn't be on the German side." Iris Elizabeth brushed an imaginary speck of dust off her spotless dress. "What about Mrs.

Bolman? Father said her parents came from Germany. Once a Hun–always a Hun."

"I remember Mrs. Bolman's mother," I said. "She was a nice old lady, but I could hardly understand a word she said. She died about two years ago. I went to the funeral in Forest Hill."

"Did she talk German?" Iris Elizabeth asked.

"I don't know. She didn't have any teeth."

"What was her name? Was it a German name?"

"Everybody called her Granny S," I said. "Why do you care what her name was?"

"If she had a German name, we'd know she was a Hun along with Rose and Della. Don't you see?"

"Rose and Della are not Huns!" I said. Dandy jumped off my lap and ran behind the tree.

Iris Elizabeth sighed and gave me a haughty look. "You don't have to yell. I'm just trying to help you face the truth."

"You don't want me to be friends with Rose and Della."

"Not true. Look, if I can prove they're German, would you still be so crazy about them? Your brother is over there fighting the Germans."

"The Bolmans are American, just like you and me. That's all there is to it." I wanted to walk away and leave Iris Elizabeth with her mean thoughts. But she was staying with us until her parents returned late from a fancy dinner and a show at the Orpheum Theater.

"Tonight after Forest Hill closes, let's go look at their grandmother's grave marker and see what her name was," Iris Elizabeth said. "That will prove it one way or another."

"It won't prove a thing. I can't believe you want to go into a cemetery at night. It's dark and kind of scary. And if the night watchman catches you, you are really in trouble. You can't even go in Forest Hill in the daytime unless you're with an adult."

"Annie, you are such a baby."

I didn't mind going into the cemetery. I'd been with the boys a bunch of times, and it was always an adventure. But I could not picture Iris Elizabeth with her pretty dress, white socks, and shiny shoes creeping through the thick underbrush in the woods around the graves.

After supper Iris Elizabeth convinced James and Robert to go to Forest Hill with us. "Let's hurry before it gets dark," she said as she started toward the road.

"Where're you going?" Robert asked.

"To Forest Hill. You said you'd go with us." Iris Elizabeth stood with her hands on her hips, glaring at Robert.

"You're just going to walk down the road and through the gate into the cemetery? Don't you know the gate's locked, and people are not allowed in after hours?" Robert shook his head and gave me a disgusted look. He was not fond of Iris Elizabeth.

"If you really want to see the cemetery tonight, Iris Elizabeth, you have to sneak in," James said. "Are you sure you want to do that?"

"You can get us in, can't you, James?" She looked up at him with the sweet, innocent face she wore around her mother.

"Of course I can. Come on." James led us through the darkening woods behind the back yard until we came to a wire fence. He held up a loose part of the fence over a hollow in the ground.

"We have to crawl under?" Iris Elizabeth complained. "My dress will get dirty."

"If you want to get into the cemetery, this is how you have to go," Robert said.

Iris Elizabeth watched as I dropped to the ground and inched my way under the fence. Robert scooted under fast as a lizard, and we stood waiting on the other side. I thought Iris Elizabeth would give up her crazy idea.

"You're sure you want to do this?" James asked.

Iris Elizabeth got to her knees and crawled under as James tried to hold the fence higher. In spite of his efforts, her satin sash snagged on the fence wire and came away with a three cornered tear.

"That's all right," she said. "It's one of my old ones." She swiped at the stains on her socks as we walked through the woods to another fence.

This time, after Robert and I climbed over, James helped Iris Elizabeth. Her shoe heel caught on the fence, and she toppled to the ground. James helped her up, and she clung to him a few seconds before she brushed herself off and went on.

After we crossed a narrow, dirt road and neared a third fence, she said, "I didn't know it would be like this. Why all these fences?"

"That was Calvary, the Catholic cemetery behind our house," Robert told her. "This one across the road is Temple Israel, the Jewish cemetery where Mr. Bolman works."

"Well, where is Forest Hill?" Iris Elizabeth had a

mud streak on her face where she had rubbed a mosquito bite.

"It's on the other side of the Jewish cemetery," James said. "We have to go over this fence and one more. Then we'll be in Forest Hill."

I had always wondered why there were so many cemeteries. When I asked Mama about it, she said some people didn't want anything to do with people that were different from them. So there were cemeteries for Catholics, Jews, or whatever, to let the dead be buried with others like them. Aunt Cal told me the cemetery for colored was way on down the road.

"Be quiet now, and don't let anybody see you," James said to Iris Elizabeth as they caught up with Robert and me. "We have to run through the graves to the other side of the Jewish cemetery."

Chapter Twelve

Like four shadows we darted from monument to monument as the darkness grew thicker. Then we were in woods again, dark woods. I could hardly see Robert's faded blue shirt ahead of me. In the muggy night air, a sticky dampness coated my skin, and the ringing buzz of cicadas sounded through the trees. Iris Elizabeth clutched the back of my dress and stumbled along behind me. Off to the left, a loud yelp and thrashing about instantly silenced the cicadas. We froze and listened to the far-off sounds of crickets and a frog.

"Must have been a couple of dogs," Robert said.

We had just started moving again when a faint whiff of skunk reached us.

"*Whew*," James said. "Glad we didn't run into that fellow."

"*Ooo*," Iris Elizabeth said. "Was that a skunk?"

"Sure was," James said. "Somebody's dog got a blast."

I wasn't near as worried about skunks as I was about where to put my bare feet. Every little rustle of grass or leaves reminded me of snakes. Daddy always said, "Snakes are more afraid of you than you are of them." Robert was probably scaring off all the snakes. But who knew about snakes?

"Here's the last fence," James whispered. "Don't make a sound. Forest Hill has a night watchman."

The fence was covered with trumpet vine, and thick bushes pressed close on the other side. James groped along until he found the hole in the fence and pulled back the vine. As Robert slipped through and held back the bushes for me, I wondered if Iris Elizabeth could make it through such a narrow opening. She did get stuck for a minute, but with James and Robert pushing and tugging at her, she managed to squeeze through.

I was surprised she had come this far. She had lost her hair bow, and her curls were tousled and hanging in her face. She had a scratch down one arm, and her clothes were a mess.

James was taken with Iris Elizabeth. He tended her like she was made of fine china. "What do you want in Forest Hill?" he asked.

"I need to see the grave of Mrs. Bolman's mother to prove something to Annie," she said.

When we came to the clearing, James whispered that I should lead because I had been to the grave. That was a long time ago, and things were different in the dark. I knew it was close to the road in the front part of the cemetery. That's where the caretaker's shelter was and probably where the night watchman would be. I ran to the nearest tall monument and crouched in its shadow. The others followed.

"What's that?" Iris Elizabeth whispered, clutching at me.

A rustling sound seemed to rise from all directions. The night was darker than ever with a tiny moon hiding behind a cloud. Gray shapes hovered near the ground and slipped through the graves, creeping, halting, starting, stopping. We were still as statues behind the monument until James's shoulders began to shake with silent laughter.

"They're rabbits," he whispered. "The graveyard rabbits."

Laughter bubbled up and out of us all. We laughed without a sound, rolling around on the ground among the gravestones, until tears poured down our faces.

When we were able to go on, I recognized a big, white monument with a huge angel on it. The grave we were looking for was between the road and that angel. I pointed, and the others all dropped down to see the name. In the shadow of a tree, the grave marker was so dark it was impossible to read. Iris Elizabeth ran her fingers over the name and then guided my finger over it. G E R T A S C H N E I D E R. Gerta Schneider. It was a German name.

In the dark I could barely see a satisfied smile on Iris Elizabeth's face as she nodded at me. That smart aleck thought she knew everything! She turned to James and said in her sugary whisper, "We can go back now, James."

At the sound of whistling, we all dropped to the ground and lay flat between graves until the night watchman passed. Then, without a sound, we ran until we reached the safety of the trees. Iris Elizabeth tripped over a marker and turned her ankle so James had to practically carry her. Somehow we made it past all the fences and back home.

I was wondering what to do about Iris Elizabeth's

appearance. With her torn clothes and scuffed shoes, she looked as scruffy as a scarecrow at the end of summer. Mama would kill us if she knew we had taken her to Forest Hill.

Daddy, Mama, and Paul John were all on the front porch with the neighbors. "James, you and Robert keep everybody on the porch while I help Iris Elizabeth get cleaned up," I said.

I might get irritated with Iris Elizabeth and her silly ideas, but I had to admire the way she took everything tonight. "We'd better hurry. My parents will be here soon," she said. "They can't see me looking like this."

Glad to have running water in the house, I turned on the kitchen faucet and wet a washrag. "I don't have time to heat it," I said. "You'll have to use it cold."

Iris Elizabeth scrubbed at her face, her arms, and her socks while I attacked her hair. I managed to comb out the leaves and twigs, but I didn't know how to make those fat curls that always lay so pretty against her collar.

"That's all right," she said. "I comb them out at night anyway."

I got a piece of cotton and a bottle of alcohol. "This is going to hurt, but I have to put some alcohol on those skinned places so you won't get a bad sore."

I thought she might blubber like a baby, but Iris Elizabeth clenched her teeth and kept quiet while I dabbed her scratches and mosquito bites with alcohol. After I tied her sash so the hole didn't show, she looked much better. There was nothing we could do about her limp from the hurt ankle, but I knew she would come up with a story to explain it.

"Why didn't you and the boys get as messed up as I did?" she said. "You did the same things I did, but you don't look any different."

"Maybe it's because we never look as good as you do in the first place."

Iris Elizabeth hugged me. "You're my true friend, Annie."

Maybe Iris Elizabeth had a little tomboy in her, too. "That was fun going to the cemetery, don't you think?" I asked.

"No!" she said with a horrified look. "I only went to prove a point. Now that you know the Bolmans are German, you can be on your guard."

"I told you they are not German, and that name does not mean a thing to me."

That night as I was drifting off to sleep, the men's voices from the porch droned on.

"...influenza over there in Europe," Mr. Adams said. "Spanish influenza...killing lots of people."

"Maybe it'll kill off all the Huns," Mr. Robinson said.

Chapter Thirteen

"It's time to go." James gave Dandy a scratch behind the ears and headed toward the road. "We don't want to be late."

"Aren't you coming with us?" Robert asked. The almost new, brown knickers that James outgrew last year fit him perfectly.

"No, I'm waiting for Mrs. Robinson and Iris Elizabeth." In my new gingham dress, I sat on the front steps and watched James and Robert walk out of sight, lunch pails in hand.

The sunny, new day was quiet. Dew crystals sparkled in the grass. This was the first day of school, and I wanted to get there early to meet Rose and Della. When Iris Elizabeth asked me to ride to school in the car, I said no. I wanted to walk with the boys as I had since first grade. The next thing I knew, Mrs. Robinson had talked Mama into letting me ride.

The Robinsons' blue sedan finally stopped in front of me, and I could not believe my eyes. Mrs. Robinson was dressed in eggplant-purple silk. She had a huge brooch glittering on her bosom and a gigantic fringed hat on her head. Iris Elizabeth wore a rose-colored silk dress, finer than any I ever saw at church, and a matching bow held back her dark curls.

"Hurry, dear, and get dressed," Mrs. Robinson

called. "I thought you would be ready."

"I am ready." I picked up my two new tablets and pencils.

Mrs. Robinson raised her eyebrows at Iris Elizabeth.

I wished I'd walked to school with James and Robert. As we drove by, boys and girls along the road turned to gape at the car, staring right at me. The minute we stopped at the school, all the early-bird students headed toward us.

"Look, those two girls have dresses like yours," Iris Elizabeth said. "Couldn't you just die?"

"No. That's Rose and Della. We bought these dresses alike to wear today."

"Come, Iris Elizabeth." Mrs. Robinson closed the car door. "I want to meet the principal and make sure she understands all your needs."

Grasping Iris Elizabeth's hand firmly, she pulled her through the gathering crowd of students who opened a path for them. "All of you keep your hands off the automobile," she said. "I don't want to see any smudges on it."

I tried to pretend I didn't know the Robinsons and just happened to get out of their car. But questions flew at me from all sides.

"Who is that girl?"

"What needs does she have?"

"How come you're riding with them, Annie?"

"Who are they?"

"They're the Robinsons," I said. "They live in that big, new house around the corner from me. Iris Elizabeth is in seventh grade, and far as I know her needs are the same as anybody else's." I pushed my way through the crowd around the car to Della and Rose, who were standing aside watching.

"So that's Iris Elizabeth," Della said. "Aren't you glad you're the one who knows her?"

"I guess, but I felt silly riding to school in a car. Have you saved many peach pits?"

"We have about half of a tow sack full," Rose said. "Herman's been helping us."

"We have a big pile of black walnuts, but we haven't taken the hulls off yet," Della said.

A tall, willowy woman with brown, wavy hair piled high on her head opened the many-paned glass doors of the new school and stepped out onto the porch. She rang a bell and we all settled down, boys scrambling into one line and girls forming another.

A blue jay feather flew over my shoulder and landed on my tablet. When I looked around, there was Charlie Dodd acting like he never saw me. Charlie was always pestering me.

I never saw a prettier school than Ford N. Taylor. The walls were the color of early spring leaves, and big windows flooded the classrooms with light. The new school smelled like paint and sawdust instead of chalk and old books.

We all trooped upstairs after the tall lady and into a big room that looked like a theater with a stage. She went up some steps onto the stage and stood beside a piano, waiting until everybody was seated. Then she struck one piano key and held a finger to her lips. When the note died, the auditorium was quiet.

"Welcome to Ford N. Taylor," she said. "I am your

principal, Miss Camilla Wainwright. I know you're all glad to be here in this fine, new school in the best country in the world. We should give thanks every day for our brave boys fighting in Europe to keep us free."

Then Katherine Wingate, a seventh grader, played the piano while we all sang *America*. I thought of Richard and sang as loud as I could, nearly bursting with pride.

When the teachers were introduced, we were surprised to hear that the sixth and seventh grades would be combined this year, with one teacher, Miss Chambers. This would be my best year yet, with a brand new school and three girlfriends in my classroom.

Miss Chambers was young, with dark, shining eyes and black curly hair twisted up on her head. She led us to our classroom where Mrs. Robinson and Iris Elizabeth were waiting. Miss Chambers was not nearly as tall as some of the boys, but she was definitely in charge. "Sixth grade will take the first three rows near the chalkboard," she said. "Seventh graders, take the other three rows. You may sit where you like in your assigned rows."

Miss Chambers was all right. Usually I had a seat in the middle of a bunch of boys. Today, I sat behind Della, and Rose sat beside me in the seventh grade section.

"I want Iris Elizabeth to sit with the little Davis girl." Mrs. Robinson's demanding voice rose over the bustle of finding seats, and the room fell silent.

Heads turned to stare at Rose and me. Rose gave me a long look, picked up her tablet, and moved to the desk beside Della. She smiled timidly at Iris Elizabeth as she came down the aisle, but Iris Elizabeth walked proudly past and took the seat next to me.

After Mrs. Robinson left, Miss Chambers explained that she would be strict and fair. "This year all the schools in the county are participating in the Liberty Seed and Nutshell Collection," she said. "There'll be a prize for the class at Ford N. Taylor that turns in the most seeds and shells to make gas masks for our soldiers overseas."

"What's the prize?" Tommy Pickens asked.

"Everybody in the winning class will march in the Liberty Pageant Parade in October," Miss Chambers said. "Each class is to choose a boy and a girl to serve as chairmen of the contest. We'll vote after morning recess."

In the hubbub of excitement about the contest, Rose and Della turned around and smiled, knowing we had a head start on collecting seeds.

At recess all the girls crowded around Iris Elizabeth to see her pretty dress and listen to her stories about Cincinnati. Even some of the boys had questions for her, mostly about the car. When I saw Rose standing alone near the steps, I inched my way through the mob around Iris Elizabeth, and Della followed. Glancing back, I saw Iris Elizabeth's glare when she noticed me with Rose and Della.

As we returned to class after recess, I watched several girls vying to walk beside Iris Elizabeth rustling along in her silk dress as she dimpled at first one and then another. Though she was full of herself, Iris Elizabeth had a charm about her that was hard to resist.

I ought to know.

When Miss Chambers called for seed chairman nominations, Robert popped out of his seat and shouted, "I nominate Rose for girls' chairman."

"Robert's sweet on Rose." Tommy Pickens laughed and puckered his lips to make noisy kissing sounds.

The boys guffawed, and Miss Chambers rang her bell to get order. "I will not tolerate such disturbances in this classroom," she said.

Rose's blushing face was half hidden by a curtain of brown hair, crimped from its everyday braids. She kept her eyes on her tablet.

Iris Elizabeth stood up. "I think we should have a seventh grade boy and a sixth grade girl to be chairmen," she said. "I nominate Robert and Annie Davis because they could work together."

Neither Robert nor I had ever been elected to anything, not even nominated, but I could hear murmurs of agreement and see heads nodding. "No. Rose would be much better than I would," I said. "Choose Rose."

"Annie's just saying that because Rose is her friend," Iris Elizabeth said.

"I nominate Billy Ray Barton for the seventh grade boy." Martha Nell, a tall, blonde seventh grader, smiled at Billy Ray.

Betty said, "Eloise should be the sixth grade girl." Eloise was her best friend, and you never saw one without the other.

On the first vote, Robert and I both were elected. Rose would have been a much better chairman than either one of us, and nobody would have voted for us if Iris Elizabeth hadn't arranged it.

Chapter Fourteen

The new lunchroom with its long tables and benches was in the basement of the school and was also used for recess on bad-weather days. One side was for boys and one for girls. At the old school, everybody had to eat on the playground or in the classroom on rainy days.

"You'll make a good seed chairman," Rose told me from across the table. "Our class is going to win that contest."

Katherine, Betty, and Eloise all said they were glad I was elected and they would bring lots of seeds. For the first time in my life, I felt like one of the girls.

Iris Elizabeth had made the others notice me. She set her pretty, little lunch basket on the table next to me and removed a linen napkin to spread out an apple, a ham sandwich, three cookies, and a piece of chocolate. Everyone else had a lunch similar to mine, cornbread and a sweet potato.

Miss Wainwright had announced that every Wednesday some mothers were coming to the school to make soup so we could have a hot meal once a week.

"Who's going to buy soup on Wednesday?" Della asked.

Eloise and Katherine said they would try the soup. Then Iris Elizabeth said, "My mother may not want me to eat that soup. You don't know what they'll put in it."

I had to squelch a smile. With remarks like that, the other girls would soon know the real Iris Elizabeth.

After school, I started toward home with Robert and some other boys. Iris Elizabeth called after me, "Annie, come back! Aren't you going to ride home with me?"

"Walk with us," I said.

"I have to wait for my mother." For the first time that day, Iris Elizabeth was alone, standing by the side of the road.

I felt sorry for her and ran back to wait with her. "How did you like Rose and Della? If you want a dress like ours, they have them at Goldsmith's. You could get a yellow one."

Iris Elizabeth gave a long sigh. "The little Huns seem nice enough."

"Don't call Rose and Della Huns," I said. "They're not."

"Mother probably wouldn't want me to wear a little dress like yours," she said. "I have a lot of new dresses for school. Mother was going to give the old ones to Cal for her daughter, but I'm sure she would let you have the nicer ones. You're a little smaller than I am, and they'd be perfect for you. You really should fix yourself up more, you know."

At the supper table that evening, while I was wondering if I wanted to wear Iris Elizabeth's fine dresses, Daddy told us President Wilson was asking people to save gas for the war by not driving their cars unless it was truly necessary.

The next morning as I left the Robinson car, I said,

"Thank you very much for giving me rides, Mrs. Robinson, but I'll be walking from now on." I had two perfectly good legs, and if Richard could be over there fighting the Germans, the least I could do was walk to school.

"Walking!" Mrs. Robinson looked like she'd tasted a green persimmon. "Nonsense, child, you'll continue to ride with us. Why would you want to walk?"

"No, ma'am. President Wilson asked people to use cars only when necessary. I will walk. Iris Elizabeth could walk with me, and you wouldn't have to drive at all."

Mrs. Robinson sat still, both hands gripping the wheel.

I leaned into the car and repeated, "Thank you for the rides, Mrs. Robinson." Then I closed the door firmly.

"I know why you want to walk," Iris Elizabeth said with a smirk. "You want to be with all those boys."

Two mornings later, she informed me that she would be walking home with me. She told her father that she'd miss some of the public school experience if she didn't walk. "He and Mother argued about it for hours," she said. "But he finally convinced her that I could make it home without her."

That afternoon, Iris Elizabeth and I were passing Forest Hill Cemetery with Robert and four other boys when James and Charlie Dodd caught up with the rest of us. "Well," Charlie said, "I see we have a girl with us today."

"I walk with you every day," I said.

"Right, Annie." Charlie snorted. "And now we

have a girl with us."

All the boys laughed as Charlie snatched my arithmetic book and pranced off. I was after him in a flash. "You give that back," I demanded as I chased him down and hit him on the shoulder.

"Make me," Charlie teased, waving the book in my face, just out of reach.

"*Ooo*! Charlie Dodd, you make me so mad." I flounced back to Iris Elizabeth, knowing he'd give back my book when he got good and ready.

Iris Elizabeth slowly shook her head and whispered, "I need to have a talk with you."

When we got home, she pulled me toward our front porch where we sat in the swing. Then she started. "Annie, I can't believe you were so uncouth on the street. I will not be seen with you if you continue to act like such a ruffian. Where did you learn your manners? From Cal?"

"Leave Aunt Cal out of this," I said. "And why do you call her plain Cal? Talk about manners. Don't you know that's disrespectful?"

"Cal is not my aunt or yours either. Mother and I think it's ignorant to call a Negro aunt." Iris Elizabeth shook her head like I was some dumb, pitiful creature. "It's your manners we're talking about," she said.

I sighed. Cincinnati must have a whole different set of rules. "If Aunt Cal had her way, I would have spent my life in the house sewing and cleaning and cooking. I never had to act like a girl because of Mama. She lost my sister, Mary, just before I was born. Then when I was three, my baby sister died at birth."

"What does that have to do with your unbecoming behavior today?" Iris Elizabeth asked.

"Mama was sick a long time after the baby died. When she got well, she said she was not losing another girl. She wanted me to be as healthy and strong as the boys so I got to do whatever they did, play and work outside mostly. And I'm glad! If I'd been treated as a girl, I never would have had so much fun."

"I see why you're the way you are," Iris Elizabeth said. "But if you want to be my true friend, you have to be a proper girl."

I could never be a girl like Iris Elizabeth, always doing and saying the right thing. "Being a girl comes easy for you and Rose and Della, but it's not easy for me."

"I'll help you." Iris Elizabeth beamed. "You stick with me, and you'll see how great being a girl can be. Didn't I already get you elected seed chairman?"

For the next few days, I worked hard at trying to change. I watched the other girls. None of them were as loud as I was, none of them acted as tough as I did, and none of them tried to outdo the boys as I did. When Della won the spelling bee and Rose came in second, they were almost apologetic about winning, instead of gloating over the win as one of the boys or I might have. I tried to be humble and quiet like the other girls.

I loved being the girls' seed chairman in the back of the room, collecting, measuring, and recording the seeds girls brought, while everybody else worked at their desks. But Miss Chambers said Robert and I were spending far too much time on the seed collection. So I made a plan with the girls. "Rose, you make a chart to show how many seeds the girls bring," I said.

Rose nodded and said, "I'll make a column for quarts and one for pecks."

"Fine," I said. "Betty, you measure the seeds and tell Martha Nell how much everybody brought. And Martha Nell, you have nice penmanship. You write it on the chart."

I noticed Martha Nell give Katherine a long look as I went on. "After the seeds are measured and recorded every day, Katherine, you can dump them all into the girls' basket in the back of the room. I'll tell Robert to do the same thing with the boys. When the baskets are full, the boys can pour all the seeds into a tow sack for the Liberty League to pick up."

I was quite pleased with the plan and with the fact that the girls were far ahead of the boys in our class, thanks to the Bolmans. "One more thing," I said. "Iris Elizabeth, you make a label that says 'Ford N. Taylor, 6th and 7th Grades,' for the tow sack."

"Yes, sir!" Iris Elizabeth clicked her heels together and stood at attention.

The girls laughed, and I pretended to laugh as a flash of heat warmed my face. They were laughing at me!

Later, Iris Elizabeth had another one of her little talks with me. "Annie," she said, "you are entirely too bossy. It's a wonder you have any friends at all."

I didn't tell her I'd never had a girlfriend except for Della and Rose, until now. "But I'm the chairman. I'm supposed to be in charge and get people to bring more seeds."

"Annie, there's more than one way to get people to do what you wish they would. I can get anything I want from anybody, even my parents. You just need to be extra nice and give them exactly what they want. For Mother and Father, I'm their perfect little girl. For boys or girls, I make them think they are something special to me. Then they do whatever I want. Try it. You'll see. It's a game."

"I know. It's like Mama says, 'You catch more flies with honey than with vinegar.'"

But somehow playing games with people seemed a little dishonest to me.

Chapter Fifteen

"You'll be happy to hear our new playground equipment is here." Miss Chambers unwrapped a brown paper parcel and handed two fat, new jump ropes to Martha Nell. "For the girls," she said.

Then she pulled out a snow-white softball, so different from the old scuffed ones we played with in the summer. She tossed it to Billy Ray and then let the paper fall off a beautiful, shiny, smooth bat. I wanted to feel its weight and the warmth of the wood in my hands. I wanted to swing that bat and feel it connect with the ball. But I was a girl. The jump ropes were for me.

On the playground Martha Nell unrolled the ropes. "Let's jump double Dutch," she said.

"No," Iris Elizabeth said. "Let's do Cinderella. Annie and I will throw first."

As usual, the girls all agreed with Iris Elizabeth. They looked at each other in surprise when I took the end of the rope. I had never played jump rope before and never wanted to. I didn't want to now, but there I stood, holding the end of the rope while one after another jumped.

Cinderella dressed in yellow
Went downtown to meet her fellow.
How many kisses did she get?

They counted and jumped until they missed. And then somebody else ran in. I twirled the rope and listened for the crack of the bat from down the hill on the boys' side of the schoolyard. That's where I wanted to be. But I had promised myself I would not get in trouble at Ford N. Taylor for going on the boys' side as I did at Oakland.

"It's our turn to jump now," Iris Elizabeth said.

Della took the rope from me, and I stood watching Iris Elizabeth jump. "...twenty-eight, twenty-nine, thirty..." the girls all chanted.

Before I knew it, I had walked away from the girls and their rope jumping, straight toward the ball field. I stood at the edge of the girls' side watching, dying to get my hands on that new bat.

"Annie, we've all had a turn." Robert came running toward me. "Do you want to try it?"

"Take a few swings, Annie," Tommy Pickens said.

I picked up the new bat, and the weight of it was perfect. I took my stance at the folded burlap bag used for home plate. Billy Ray tossed me the ball and I swung, hitting the ball just over second base. What a great feeling! I wanted to hit again and again.

"How is the new bat?" Miss Chambers called from the top of the hill.

I had done it again. I was on the boys' side. I wanted to curl into a tiny ball like a roly-poly bug and roll away.

Miss Chambers walked down the hill and reached for the bat. I was in trouble now. "Throw me one," she said.

Billy Ray tossed her a nice easy one, and she hit it

way over the heads of everybody. She hit it farther than Charlie Dodd could, clear out to the edge of the schoolyard. Who would believe a pretty little lady like Miss Chambers could smack a ball like that?

"Wow!"

"Hit it again, Miss Chambers."

A couple of boys chased after the ball, and the others crowded around the teacher and me.

"No, it's time to go in now," she said as she started up the hill. "Annie, I'll see you after school."

I was in trouble for being on the boys' side, but I didn't feel bad about it. Miss Chambers would understand.

The problem was the other girls didn't.

Iris Elizabeth frowned at me and shook her head like I was a disgrace. As we lined up to go in, Della caught my hand and whispered, "I thought you were going to act like a girl this year."

The classroom emptied quickly after school with happy shouts from the boys and a few backward glances at me from the girls. I sat in my seat waiting until Miss Chambers looked up from her paperwork. "Annie, you know you cannot go on the boys' side of the playground."

I nodded.

"I know how you feel," she said. "I was a bit of a tomboy myself, and I had a hard time staying with the girls at school. But rules are rules. I don't want to see you on the boys' side again."

"I hate jumping rope."

"You don't have to jump rope, Annie. But you must stay where you belong." Miss Chambers picked up her red marking pen. "Now help me check these spelling papers, and then you can go."

I was relieved to see Iris Elizabeth, Katherine, and Martha Nell sitting on the bench under the oak tree when I came out. I was relieved until I saw their severe looks of disapproval. They must have been taking lessons from Miz Lizzie.

Iris Elizabeth put such stock in proper behavior that she might not be my friend any more. If she didn't want me around, none of the other girls would either, except Rose and Della. I loved being Iris Elizabeth's friend and having the other girls talk to me. Maybe Iris Elizabeth did say mean things sometimes, but I was getting used to her. And I didn't mind pretending I liked the same girly things she did.

"Thanks for waiting with me," Iris Elizabeth said as Martha Nell and Katherine headed down Alice Avenue. "We'll see you tomorrow."

She said *we* so she couldn't be too mad at me. She took my arm. "Annie, I can't keep smoothing things over with the other girls. You have to act like one of us if you want to be part of the group. It's for your own good."

"I know." I tried to look ashamed. But I was glad I saw Miss Chambers hit that ball. And I was glad I got to try the new bat. Being a proper girl was no fun.

Just the two of us walking home together without the jokes and teasing of the boys seemed strange. Nobody else was on the road, and Iris Elizabeth had nothing more to say until we came to the Jewish cemetery. Mr. Bolman was standing just outside the gate with two other men. "Look, there's Mr. Bolman," she said. "Wonder what he's doing there."

"You know that's where he works," I said.

"*Shh*! Don't let him see us." She pulled me behind a tree beside the road and peered around it. "He's giving them some papers. Maybe it's spy information."

"Come on. You're being silly." I marched on down the road with Iris Elizabeth running to catch up.

Mr. Bolman disappeared inside the cemetery, and we passed the other men talking in low, guttural tones as they studied the papers.

"Did you hear that?" Iris Elizabeth whispered. "They were speaking in German!"

Chapter Sixteen

"Annie, Annie!" Paul John yelled as he ran down the road toward Iris Elizabeth and me. "We got a letter from Richard!"

I forgot Iris Elizabeth and raced toward home. I snatched up the open letter from the kitchen table, and read it, loving the angular slant of Richard's writing. My special note said he was glad I was learning to be a young lady, but he might not know me if I wasn't a tomboy when he got back.

Mama was smiling as she put a cake into the oven. "We're celebrating! Richard's all right!" she said. "He thinks the war will be over soon, and he can be home by Christmas."

That was the good news in the letter. Richard also said he was in a battle, and about a fourth of the soldiers in his platoon were injured or lost. He had never been so scared. I remembered my dream and knew exactly how he felt.

The next morning Della and I lined up behind Rose. Miss Wainwright rang the bell, and the long line of girls started into the building. Iris Elizabeth broke into line behind me, grabbed my shoulder, and whispered, "Have you heard?"

"Heard what?"

"Not so loud," she said. "The Bolmans will hear

you." She pulled me aside to let the line pass.

"What are you talking about?"

"Last night over on the river, two men were caught trying to blow up a barge loaded with army trucks. You know what that means."

"No, I don't."

"Mr. Bolman," she said. "He was in on the plot. Didn't we see him yesterday giving the plans to two Germans?"

"He gave some papers to two men speaking German, but that doesn't mean they're the ones who tried to blow up the barge. They were probably buying cemetery lots. How did you hear about the barge anyway?"

"Somebody telephoned my father last night," she said. "Don't you think it's very suspicious? Father thought so when I told him about Mr. Bolman and the two men."

Talk about the barge was flying around the school, and I could not concentrate on lessons that day. At lunch, I chattered away to Della and Rose about Richard's letter and the seed collecting so they wouldn't hear the rumors about their father.

That afternoon I was fuming when Iris Elizabeth and I lagged behind the boys to talk. "How can you think Mr. Bolman would have anything to do with blowing up a bunch of army trucks headed for the war?" I said. "He loves this country."

"So he says." Iris Elizabeth tossed her head and walked faster.

"He buys Liberty Bonds. How many bonds has your father bought?"

"Father says money is tight now," Iris Elizabeth said. "He's going to buy some as soon as he can."

"You can't think the Bolmans are not loyal. Rose, Della, and Herman brought in two tow sacks of nuts and seeds this morning, more than anybody else. Della said they worked till dark yesterday hulling black walnuts."

"I wondered why their fingers were black," Iris Elizabeth said. "You wouldn't catch me ruining my hands like that."

"That's why I don't see how you can accuse the Bolmans. They do all they can to help in the war effort."

"That's the way spies work. They try to look innocent. If you don't believe me, just forget it. You'll see." Iris Elizabeth gave me an all-knowing look and changed the subject. "Come home with me now, and choose the dresses you want. Mother wants to give the others to Cal tomorrow."

Surely, Iris Elizabeth didn't really think Mr. Bolman was a spy. She was just talking. She had to be.

We were spending more and more time together. Every afternoon I rushed through my chores at home, usually with her watching and waiting while I ironed Daddy's shirts, peeled potatoes, or did whatever else Mama needed done. Iris Elizabeth never pitched in to help as Della would have, but I didn't expect her to work. It was enough for me that she was there talking and laughing while I worked. When I finished, we would do our homework at her house where Aunt Cal always had lemonade and cookies for us.

Mrs. Robinson expected me to come over there all the time now and made me feel like I belonged. The day Iris Elizabeth gave me her old dresses, Mrs. Robinson parked herself on the settee and made me try on dress after dress. "That one is perfect with your hair," she said. "That high waistline does nothing for you. Try the blue silk."

She decided eight dresses were right for my coloring and were most becoming on me. Until that day I'd been glad to wear any dress that wasn't too tight or too big, never thinking about what it did for me besides cover my nakedness.

The next week I stood before the open chifforobe, choosing a dress to wear to the theater with the Robinsons. I had never had so many dresses, and they all looked new.

"Annie, that's way too many dresses for any one girl," Mama said, as she watched me hold up one dress and then another.

"I thought about giving Della and Rose each one, but Iris Elizabeth wouldn't like that."

"I guess not." Mama held the overskirt of a peach-colored satin up to her cheek. "This is the one I like."

"I wish it was your size," I said. Mama seldom got anything new or pretty.

That night, riding downtown in the Robinsons' car, I felt like Cinderella going to the ball in a beautiful satin dress. I had never been to the Orpheum Theater before. Brilliant crystal chandeliers sparkled overhead. Gold leaf and heavy plush draperies decorated the galleries and the stage. I was gazing at the elaborate scene embroidered on the big curtain across the stage when Mrs. Robinson whispered in my ear, "Dear, you mustn't gawk."

Embarrassed, I looked around to see who else had noticed me acting like a curious goose, but all those beautiful people in their fancy clothes were chatting away, intent on their own business. So I relaxed and followed Iris Elizabeth to our seats, breathing in the delicious perfumes of ladies we passed.

I loved that stage full of singing and dancing performers in those wonderful costumes. The most amazing thing was the Golden Bird. It was a little canary that could sing any tune a lady played on a violin. Iris Elizabeth acted like the evening was nothing special, but to me it was magic.

When I first started going places with the Robinsons, Mama was glad for me. She said I needed to learn how to conduct myself in social situations. After a while though, she began telling me I was spending too much time with the Robinsons.

The day we went to the harness races, I was wearing a dark blue dress with a dropped waist and a sailor collar. Mrs. Robinson expected me to look nice when I went out with them, and that meant wearing one of Iris Elizabeth's dresses. When I arrived at their house, the blue ribbon matching the dress was perched atop my wild mass of coppery curls.

Mrs. Robinson stared at me and shook her head. "Cal," she said, "see if you can do something with her hair."

"Yes, ma'am," Aunt Cal said. "I been fixing this chile's hair since she was born."

"Now, Cal, I don't want a child's hair style," Mrs.

Robinson said. "If she's to be seen with us, she needs to be properly groomed. Give her some finger waves around the face and a cascade of curls in the back."

"Oh, I don't know," Aunt Cal said. "I don't think I can do that."

She turned to me. "What would your mama say? Her little girl with grown-up hair."

"Just do it, Cal." Mrs. Robinson's voice coming out of my mouth stunned Aunt Cal. And me, too. The hurt look on Aunt Cal's face pierced my soul, and I wanted to jump up and hug her, but I didn't. The Robinsons were there.

Chapter Seventeen

When Iris Elizabeth held the mirror for me to see my new look, I could not believe that fine looking girl was me. Iris Elizabeth had been dabbing lemon juice on my freckles every afternoon since school started, and now they hardly showed. I felt like a lovely young lady until I got home after the races that night.

Mama hit the ceiling. "Girl, what have you done to yourself?" she said. "You don't look like anybody I know. You're spending far too much time with the Robinsons. I want you at home more, you hear?"

"But, Mama, you wanted me to be a young lady."

"A young lady, yes, but not some kind of high-falutin' patootie I don't even know. You just cool your friendship with Iris Elizabeth. She is not your type."

"But, Mama, she is. I'm the kind of girl she likes."

"I'm not talking about it any more. Just behave yourself and act your age. With that hair you look like a twenty-year-old. Now get to bed."

Mama just didn't want me to be with the Robinsons. She never had liked them since the day Mrs. Robinson shut the door on us. She thought I should stay at home and work all the time like she did. Mama did not understand. She had never worn pretty dresses and gone to the theater and places.

My time with the Robinsons was different,

exciting. People noticed me. They never had before. I was becoming a young lady, one with good manners and good grooming. Even my fingernails were smooth ovals now instead of the jagged messes they had been.

Yet, another part of me longed for the old days when I was like one of the boys. With Iris Elizabeth I could never run down a hill so fast I felt I was flying or let out a whoop of joy just for the fun of it.

Early Saturday I woke to the sound of dishes and pots rattling in the kitchen. Today Mama was going across town to visit her sister, and she bustled about the kitchen faster and louder than usual.

"Now, Annie," she said, "you stay here and catch up on your schoolwork while we're gone. I don't want you going over to the Robinsons today. You need some time away from Iris Elizabeth. If we don't get back before supper, there's potato salad in the icebox and pinto beans cooking on the stove. You can slice some tomatoes and put out some of that rye bread and a little ham."

Mama and Paul John walked down to the car stop on Hernando to wait for the streetcar. Daddy had gone to look at some tools with Mr. Adams. The boys were all off somewhere, and I was alone in the house.

Dandy lay purring in my lap as I sat rocking in Mama's chair. Mama lived in that kitchen, working all the time. Her sewing basket was piled high with holey socks, and shirts with lost buttons waited beside the rocker. If Mama were home, she would be preserving the figs she picked before she left, and we'd be ironing the clothes we washed yesterday. Poor Mama did nothing but work. Even her fun was work. Today she would help Aunt Lou stretch a finished quilt top on the quilting frame over cotton batting. Then they would sit around the frame all afternoon making tiny stitches.

Mrs. Robinson only went into the kitchen to tell Aunt Cal what to do. Next to her parlor, she had a sitting room where she would listen to music on the Victrola and do a little fancy embroidery if she felt like it. Or she would sit upstairs at a golden oak secretary and write letters filled with her spidery script. She visited friends in town, and I'll bet they didn't work when she got there either. Mrs. Robinson was the only woman I knew who didn't work herself to death.

I looked down at the book I had to read for school. I didn't care about Tom Sawyer and his troubles with Aunt Polly. I had troubles of my own. Mama wanted me to grow up and be just like her. Being a lady was hard enough. I certainly was not going to be a household drudge like all the women in the neighborhood, except Mrs. Robinson.

Robert burst into the house yelling, "Annie! Annie! Come on. Charlie wants you for the team."

For a second, I was ready to dash out of the house. Then I remembered. "Robert, you know I don't play ball any more."

"*Aww*, Annie, you don't do anything any more." Robert was my best buddy, and I hadn't seen much of him lately. "You don't go down to the creek with me. You don't play hide and seek in the evenings. You don't even talk to Rose and Della."

"I do talk to Rose and Della."

"That's not what Rose says. She told me none of the girls at school, including you, have anything to do with her and Della since we heard about the Hun barge plot."

"You mean they know about that?" I felt terrible, knowing I hadn't paid much attention to Della or Rose since that day of rumors about Mr. Bolman.

"Of course, they know! They're not deaf or stupid. Some friend you are. The Bolmans are being treated like they shot the preacher, and you don't even know it."

It was true. When I was with Iris Elizabeth and the other girls, I was so elated that I scarcely gave Della or Rose a thought. I was a rotten friend.

"Here, Annie, put on these pants and come on." Robert held out a pair of his old pants that I used to wear when I played with the boys.

"You know Mama said I couldn't play with you boys. What would the other girls think if they saw me playing ball?"

"Mama's not here. She won't know. Nobody will. Those boys from Whitehaven are at the school saying they can beat any team we come up with. Annie, we need you to play."

More than anything I wanted to go with Robert and forget about being a girl. But I couldn't spoil my new life. Yet…it was a perfect day for a ball game, sunny and not too hot. Nobody would know, and Mama didn't say not to play ball.

I snatched the pants from Robert and pulled them on over my old dress that bunched up around my hips as it always had when I wore pants.

When Robert and I trotted onto the field behind the school, Charlie Dodd ran to meet us. "You got her!"

He handed me the ball. "Here, Annie, warm up with Robert."

"A girl!" Fred, a new boy who lived on the other side of the school, gave me a disgusted look.

"We don't play with girls," Fred's brother Danny said. "If she plays, we're not."

"All right," Charlie said. "You can play for the other team if you want to. Annie's our pitcher."

I had never played with any boys except the ones in the neighborhood. The team from Whitehaven laughed and hooted when we took the field with me on the pitcher's mound.

"That's okay," Charlie said as he patted me on the back. "You can do it."

My first pitch was a wild one, way over the head of Tommy Pickens who was catching. The other team hooted and howled.

"I can pitch better than that. Let me try," Fred yelled. "We need a pitcher."

"Shut up, Fred," Billy Ray yelled from first base. "Show 'em, Annie."

The other team got two hits before I settled down. When the first inning was over, I felt much better. The score was three to two, their favor, but I knew we could beat that team.

By the end of the fourth inning, catcalls from the other bench had stopped, and I had five strikeouts. The pitcher for the other team was not that great, but they had some big boys that could knock the stuffing out of the ball. Our fielders managed to snag most of the flies and throw out three runners at the plate.

We were ahead in the last inning, six to five with

two outs, when their best hitter came up. Runners were on first and second. I told Charlie I was a little tired, but he said he wanted me to keep pitching if I could because the team was sizzling with everybody where they were. A red spot on my finger was becoming a blister. I blew on it and gripped the ball for my windup.

Chapter Eighteen

The instant the ball left my hand, I knew I'd misfired. It shot back into my leg just above the ankle, and I fell to the ground. My leg hurt so bad I couldn't move. Infielders pounded toward me, and the batter was headed for first. I gritted my teeth, squeezed back the tears, and rolled over to snatch the ball from a pile of dust. My weak throw toward first was just in time for Billy Ray to tag the batter as he ran by.

We won! The boys crowded around me slapping each other on the back. "We did it! We did it! Way to go, Annie!"

"You all right?" James pulled me to my feet.

"Here, I'll carry her," Charlie said. "She won the game."

Next thing I knew, I was riding on Charlie Dodd's shoulders, surrounded by the rest of the team. They bragged and boasted, as boys do, about how we showed that Whitehaven team. It had been a glorious victory, and my leg was feeling much better by the time we got home.

There sat Iris Elizabeth in the swing on our front porch, her eyes glued to me. She was stroking a cat in her lap, a cream-colored cat with dark brown ears and tail. The noisy crowd of boys dumped me on the swing beside her, and my bubble of joy and excitement burst under the gaze of those green eyes.

"You really came through for us," Billy Ray said.

"Take care of that leg, Annie," Charlie called. And the boys were gone, without giving one bit of notice to Iris Elizabeth.

Taking the cat, she moved to a cane-bottomed chair by the wall and continued to scrutinize me. "You're filthy!" she said.

Covered with dust, my dress blousing over Robert's ragged pants, I looked nothing like Iris Elizabeth's friend. Mrs. Robinson would not let such a grubby person in the house, and neither would Mama. I pulled down my sock. It was brown with dirt.

Iris Elizabeth gasped when she saw the bruise. It looked worse than I expected. The stitching on the ball was clearly visible in the purple and blue imprint on my leg. No wonder it hurt so bad!

"Why did you do it?" Iris Elizabeth stared at me with a look of disdain.

"I don't know. I guess I'm just a tomboy." The glory of victory had vanished. I had spoiled everything as surely as a slug leaving its slime on ripe strawberries.

"I want you to meet Lady Jasmin." Iris Elizabeth smoothed the cat's long tail. "She's a Siamese."

"You mean you're not mad at me?"

"The way I see it is you had to have one last lapse into your old ways. But I'll tell you something, Annie. If you can't be a proper girl now, this is the end of our friendship. The very end."

"I can be a proper girl. You know I can."

"You'd better be. If you're not, I'll take Katherine

Wingate for my best friend."

Iris Elizabeth reluctantly took piano lessons from Katherine's mother once a week. I could just see Katherine Wingate in my place next to Iris Elizabeth, with all the other girls crowded around. I would be alone, on the outside again.

"Why'd you pick me anyway?" I said. "I can't do anything right."

"Annie, you're like a starburst in the Fourth of July sky–loud, exciting, and full of surprises. Mother thinks you're beautiful. She thinks Katherine is plain."

Thank goodness! Iris Elizabeth was not dropping me. The Robinsons were as foreign and fascinating to me as that Siamese cat, but they were part of my life. I was part of theirs, and I intended to keep it that way.

When I reached out to pet the Siamese, her blue eyes shone up at me, and she let out a long, low meow that sounded like, "How are you?"

"Did you hear that? She talks," I said.

"Yes, she does." Iris Elizabeth stroked the cat with pride. "Lady Jasmin was a tiny kitten when Mother bought her the last time we were in Cincinnati. My uncle brought her to me last night. Isn't she the most elegant cat you've ever seen? Look at her collar. It's a rhinestone bracelet. Mother got one just like it for Dandy." Iris Elizabeth pulled another bracelet out of her pocket and handed it to me.

"Lady Jasmin is a gorgeous cat," I said. "And the rhinestone collar is perfect for her. But I don't know about Dandy."

"I think you should call him Dandelion. That is what you named him, and it sounds so much more sophisticated than Dandy."

Just what I needed, a sophisticated alley cat. I didn't want a fancy collar for Dandy, but Iris Elizabeth would get mad if I refused.

When I showed Robert that rhinestone collar, I thought he would never stop laughing. "Dandy can't wear that," he said. "He's a tom."

"I know that, but Iris Elizabeth thinks he should have a fine collar like her cat."

"Forget Iris Elizabeth. If you want a collar for Dandy, make him a leather one fit for a tom. I have some leather strings you can braid."

I put the rhinestone bracelet beside the blue jay feather from Charlie Dodd in the little wooden box Daddy made for my treasures and stuck it in the bottom of the chifforobe. I'd tell Iris Elizabeth that Dandy would wear it only for special because, being an outside cat, he might lose it.

Mama jumped all over me when she saw my bruise. "Girl, I don't know what I'm going to do with you. You're either trying to be another Mrs. Mary Robinson or you want to kill yourself playing with the boys."

"I won't play with the boys again, Mama. I promise."

"I'm not so sure I wouldn't rather have you stay a tomboy than see you living and breathing the Robinsons. Those people are a bad lot, and I don't want you around them."

"Mama, the Robinsons are not bad. They're just different. Don't you want me to be a proper lady?"

"Not if you think Mrs. Robinson is a proper lady, I

don't!" Mama fastened the glass top on the last of the fig preserves and slammed the jar so hard onto the worktable I was afraid it would break.

"Annie, you listen to your Mama," Daddy said from behind his newspaper.

The bruise on my leg throbbed with pain that night as I lay in bed, thinking of the fun I had playing ball with the boys. I felt more alive during that game than I ever had with Iris Elizabeth. But I was a girl and had to act like one.

Monday morning I dressed for school with special care in one of the silk dresses Iris Elizabeth gave me, a leaf green, long-waisted one with a dark green sash. I wanted her to forget seeing me in my dirty, sloppy ball-playing clothes.

Daddy was gone, and the boys were almost through breakfast by the time I got into the kitchen.

Paul John stared at me and licked off a milk mustache. "*Ooo*! Annie, you're pretty."

"Where'd you get that outfit?" Robert asked. "From Iris Elizabeth, I bet. If you don't watch, you'll be as crazy as she is."

"Dear, don't you think that dress is a little too much for school?" Mama spread jelly on a half eaten biscuit from Paul John's plate and popped it into her mouth. She never ate breakfast until the rest of us were through. "You could put on one of those dresses you got from Susan Dodd or that green gingham we bought before school started."

"Oh, Mama, those are so ordinary," I said. "Iris Elizabeth always wears dresses like this to school. You want me to look pretty, don't you?"

"Pretty is as pretty does." Mama slammed the biscuit pan down on the worktable.

Feeling very conspicuous in Iris Elizabeth's dress, I walked to school with James and Robert, wondering if Elvie felt as uncomfortable in Iris Elizabeth's dresses as I did. The only time I wanted to wear one was when I went out with the Robinsons, and even then I didn't feel like myself in such fine clothes. As we rounded the corner, shouts and angry voices erupted from a crowd in front of the school.

"What's going on?" James took off down the road toward the commotion.

I raced after him and Robert. That troublesome bow flew out of my hair, and I had to stop and pick it up. Then I ran as fast as I could toward the school where a crowd had gathered by the road. Mr. Bolman was lowering a full tow sack from his wagon to the ground.

"Get out of here, Hun!"

"Go back to Germany!"

"Hun lover!"

A menacing mob of boys surrounded Mr. Bolman. Ralph Marshall, the biggest, meanest boy in eighth grade, and two other boys kept pushing Mr. Bolman until he fell against the wagon.

"Rose, Della, Herman, get into the building. Now," Mr. Bolman shouted, his accent stronger than ever. With his head he motioned toward the school building just as Ralph Marshall punched him in the face and knocked him into the wagon wheel. Mr. Bolman never tried to hit any of the boys. Shielding his face, he turned his back to a barrage of punches from Ralph and the others and managed to climb into the wagon. He struggled into the seat and picked up the reins. Dolly began to move forward. Mr. Bolman looked back and stopped the horse.

A stitch in my side gave me such a pain I had to slow down and walk. I thought Mr. Bolman should drive away as fast as he could, but he just sat there looking back at his children surrounded by that unruly mob of boys.

Ralph Marshall reached into the tow sack and pulled out a handful of black walnuts. He threw them at Mr. Bolman, hitting him on the back. "Dirty, rotten Hun!"

Other boys loaded up and pelted Mr. Bolman with walnuts. "Let me at him!"

"We'll teach you!"

The shouts died, and the only sound was the thud of walnuts pounding the back and head of Mr. Bolman.

A shrill cry rang out as Rose hurled herself at the boys. "No, no, stop it! Stop, you'll hurt him!"

Herman and Della rushed into the fray, grabbing walnuts, and Della flung herself over the tow sack to keep the boys away from them.

James, with Robert close behind, reached the scene. "What do you think you're doing?" James yelled, placing himself between Mr. Bolman and the boys.

"Get out of the way, Davis," Ralph Marshall said. "You don't know what this Hun tried to do."

Miss Wainwright, followed by all the teachers and Mr. Denton, the custodian, ran across the schoolyard ringing her bell. "Order! Order! We must have order," she said. "Students, line up and proceed into the building. Go to your classrooms at once."

Most of the students obeyed and formed two lines. Only a few angry boys still muttering about what would happen to Huns around there were left. Robert was helping Della and Herman pick up spilled walnuts. Rose stood with her hands on her hips, glaring at the boys as they walked toward the building.

As Ralph Marshall and two of his friends stalked down the hill behind the school, Mr. Denton said to Mr. Bolman, "I'll keep an eye on the youngsters for you, John. Don't you worry about a thing."

"I'll be here when school is out. Just keep them safe till I come," Mr. Bolman said. He nodded to Rose, Della, and Herman. Then he touched Dolly with the reins and drove on by me, his face ravaged with distress.

Tears poured down Della's cheeks. I put my arms around her, and she was trembling like a leaf in a windstorm. "Why were they so mad?" she said. "Daddy didn't do anything."

I could not answer.

Chapter Nineteen

Robert and Herman pulled the sack of walnuts to the school building. I followed with Rose and Della, an arm around each of them. In the classroom everybody stopped talking and stared at us as we went to our desks. Her face down, half hidden by her hair, Della could not stop crying. I patted her on the back and gave her my handkerchief. Rose reached across the aisle to hold her hand.

Iris Elizabeth minced in just before class began and gave me a big smile as she slid her books into her desk. I could not bear to look at her. She had never liked the Bolmans, and Mr. Robinson was always talking against Mr. Bolman.

At recess I wanted to be with Rose and Della, but the other girls crowded around me, admiring my dress.

"Annie, I never realized how beautiful you are," Betty said.

"That's a lovely dress. Where did you get it?" Martha Nell said.

Iris Elizabeth stood beside me like a proud grandmother. She had made me promise I wouldn't tell that the dresses came from her. "Martha Nell, where are your manners?" she said. "Don't you know you never ask a lady the origin of her clothing? You just admire." She turned to me and said, "You look very nice, Annie."

Of course, the girls knew exactly where I got the dress, and I didn't care. I was accustomed to wearing other people's clothes.

I finally escaped from the other girls, and found Rose and Della alone in the classroom. "It'll be all right," I said. "Nobody could ever really believe your daddy would support the Germans."

"Some people must," Rose said as her stony eyes met mine. "They tried to hurt him, and he'd never harm a flea."

"I was so scared," Della said. "Poor Daddy! I hope nothing like that ever happens again." Tears flowed from her swollen red eyes.

"It won't. It'll all blow over and be forgotten. You wait and see," I said. But I wondered if it would. I felt like a traitor wearing Iris Elizabeth's dress.

That afternoon I was smoldering inside as I watched Iris Elizabeth practice her wiles on the boys we walked with. For once, the boys, full of talk about the attack on Mr. Bolman, ignored her attempts to charm. I never said anything until the boys had scattered. Then I exploded. "Iris Elizabeth, you don't even care about what happened to Mr. Bolman. He could have been injured. What's the matter with you?"

Wide-eyed, Iris Elizabeth said, "Why would I care what happens to a Hun?" She tore off the bright orange blossoms of a butterfly weed that grew beside the road and let them drift through her fingers to the ground. "My uncle says people in Cincinnati don't tolerate Germans or Hun lovers. And Father says he doesn't know why they do here."

She linked her arm with mine. I felt like pulling away, but she held tight and leaned closer. "Let's talk about something nice," she said. "Annie, I haven't had a chance to tell you. Mother said I could have the girls in the class over for tea on a Sunday afternoon. You'll help me plan it, won't you?"

Iris Elizabeth didn't see the attack on Mr. Bolman, and she probably didn't know how serious it was. She was my friend, and she wouldn't mean any harm to the Bolmans. She just wanted me to stop associating with them. Maybe at the tea she would see how nice Rose and Della really were.

"A tea like your mother and her friends have? I wouldn't know what to do," I said.

"That's why we're having the tea, so you can learn. Mother says she wants my friends, especially you, to know how ladies entertain."

A few days later, as the girls in our class clustered under the oak tree in the schoolyard, Iris Elizabeth told them about the Sunday tea. "You'll get an invitation soon," she said.

What is a tea anyway?" Eloise asked.

"You'll like it," Iris Elizabeth said. "You get to eat all the sweets and cakes you want."

The other girls laughed, and Eloise's face flamed as she smoothed her dress over her ample stomach.

I hated the way Iris Elizabeth made remarks like that to everybody. She pretended she didn't know their feelings were hurt. Then she'd say something to make them think she really cared about them.

Betty, who was even thinner than Rose, asked, "What do you do at a tea besides eat?"

"Oh! That's the fun part of it," Iris Elizabeth said. "You dress up in your best and sit around talking and laughing while you have the tea and sweets. My friends in Cincinnati were always having teas."

"I hope my mother will let me go," Martha Nell said. "She says Sunday is for relatives, and mine always come."

"It's a long way to your house for some people, Iris Elizabeth." I was thinking of Rose and Della. "If parents bring them in the buggy, could the parents be at the tea, too?"

"Heavens, no," Iris Elizabeth said. "My mother is right. You people are so rural. Parents would spoil the tea. It's for girls only."

As our class was filing in after recess, the first graders were coming out. "Where are the Huns?" a little voice chirped. "I want to see the Huns."

Some in our class chuckled, and Tommy Pickens pointed to Rose and Della at the end of the girls' line, far behind anybody else.

"Hush, Nathan! That's not a nice thing to say," the first grade teacher said.

But it was too late. Rose and Della had heard every word, and Della's tears flowed again as she reached for Rose. Since the walnut throwing, the Bolmans had stayed to themselves. The harassing was not open enough for the teachers to see it, but it was constant. Except for Robert, the boys in our class made a big issue of turning away when Rose or Della walked by, and most of the girls were just as bad. Name-calling, glares, and gestures followed the sisters through the halls and the schoolyard.

I let the other girls pass so I could walk with Rose and Della. "Don't let it bother you." I put my arm around Della. "Just ignore them."

"Don't you think we try?" Rose said bitterly. "It's hard to ignore something that happens over and over and over again."

"And we didn't do a thing to them," Della said. "I thought they were my friends."

Della had always been surrounded by friends until Iris Elizabeth came. Trying to cheer her up, I asked, "Do you think you'll be going to the tea? It sounds like fun, don't you agree?"

"I don't know," Della said. She was so different now. She had always been ready to laugh and have fun. Now she seemed to be crying most of the time.

Rose stared stonily ahead with a pinched look on her face. "It could be fun, if things were different."

"I hate the war," I said. "People are so ugly and mean. I want you two to be happy, and I want Richard home."

The war was always with us. Miss Chambers read newspaper articles to the class and showed big cartoon pictures of soldiers and tanks on the front page. In one day about twenty-one thousand Memphis men signed up for the war draft. The Allies were pushing the Germans back to Germany. A new law requiring every man between the ages of eighteen and forty-five to join the army or work at some other job was passed. A type of influenza was killing soldiers in our army and the German army, too. The worst part was the list of soldiers lost or missing. I worried about Richard and prayed every day that his name wouldn't be on that list.

After we heard two hundred peach seeds were needed to make one gas mask, James, Robert, and I worked harder than ever to collect seeds. We scoured the ground under the trees in McKenzie's peach orchard. Our soldiers needed gas masks more than ever with the chemicals the Germans were using.

Though the evenings were getting shorter, the neighbor men still gathered on the porch to talk about the war. I couldn't help listening until Mama caught me and sent me in the house.

One day I picked up Dandy and stood near the porch, holding him in my arms. Mr. Dodd tipped his chair back against the wall and sprinkled tobacco onto a paper to roll a cigarette. "Have you heard about The Huncrusher?" he said.

"You mean that big tank they made here in Memphis?" Mr. Adams swatted at a mosquito buzzing around his head. "It's going to be in the Liberty Pageant parade down Main Street."

"I've seen it. The biggest tank ever," Mr. Robinson said. "It should teach the Germans and the Hun lovers that we mean business."

Chapter Twenty

Iris Elizabeth and I were in her mother's upstairs sitting room writing invitations to the tea. Iris Elizabeth counted out lacy, white folded cards with her name engraved on the front. "We only need six invitations and one more for you," she said.

"But we have ten girls in our class."

"You don't think I'm inviting Rose and Della, do you? My parents wouldn't let them in the house. How many girls do you think would come if they knew the Bolman girls would be here?"

"Well, I won't be here if they're not. Just keep your old invitations, and your tea and cakes. I'm going home." I stormed out of the upstairs sitting room and down the stairs.

As I ran through the foyer, Mrs. Robinson called, "Slow down, Annie dear."

She came after me, holding her embroidery in one hand. "You're forgetting young ladies do not run through the house."

"I am not and never have been a young lady." I wanted to ram my fist through that white calla lily in the stained glass of the door.

"You seem to be upset, dear. Come, sit with me in the parlor." Mrs. Robinson put her arm around my shoulder and firmly guided me toward the parlor. "Cal, bring us a pot of tea. And tell Iris Elizabeth to come down."

I didn't want to sit down with a pot of tea and pretend to be a lady, but I didn't want to aggravate Mrs. Robinson either.

Mrs. Robinson and I were seated in front of a fancy silver tea set and a plate of pastries when she said, "Tell me, dear, what is the problem?"

I had never felt she was concerned about my problems, and I still didn't think she was. But she did ask.

"Rose and Della won't get an invitation to the tea," I said, "and next to Iris Elizabeth, they're my best friends."

"Oh, that," Mrs. Robinson said, dismissing the thought with a flip of her hand. She poured hot tea into delicate china cups and, with a tiny pair of silver tongs, dropped a couple of sugar cubes into each. "We were afraid you wouldn't understand. You know we have to consider our position in this community and invite into our home only those of most outstanding character."

"I'm not outstanding," I said. "Nobody even noticed me before Iris Elizabeth came."

"That's exactly why we thought you'd be grateful for a social occasion to display the manners you've developed as a result of your friendship with Iris Elizabeth," Mrs. Robinson said. "Now you can not compare with Iris Elizabeth, but I am very pleased with your progress."

She thought I should be just like Iris Elizabeth. I could never be a devious sneak like her.

Iris Elizabeth, wearing her perfect little girl face,

had been listening at the door. "Mother and I planned the tea mainly for you," she said, "so everybody will know you're my best friend. We went to a lot of trouble for you so you have to come."

Now I knew Iris Elizabeth had persuaded her mother to have the tea by pretending it was for me. For some reason, Mrs. Robinson had taken a fancy to me, and I did not want to lose her favor. I had seen her anger burst forth like a summer hailstorm pelting a petunia bed after Aunt Cal accidentally crossed her.

After two cups of tea, three cookies, and a lot of talk, I finally left, with Iris Elizabeth and her mother thinking I accepted what they said about the Bolmans. I was turning into another Iris Elizabeth.

Walking home from school the next day, Iris Elizabeth gave me another one of her for-your-own-good talks. "Annie," she said, "can't you understand that if you keep hovering around the Bolmans, people will associate you with the Huns?"

"So what?" Poor Della and Rose. Hardly anybody talked to them at school. Even I had a hard time staying friends with them.

Iris Elizabeth sighed. "Annie, you are the kind of girl who could go far. See how much better you look now. Your hair, your nails, certainly your clothes. Mother says you have a lot of potential."

I looked up at the one fluffy white cloud in a clear blue sky. A few yellow and gold maple leaves lay on the ground, and I kicked my way through them.

Iris Elizabeth continued, "The fact is I cannot be your friend if you are a recognized Hun lover. It would rub off on me. Don't you know if you associate with

Huns, people will consider you a Hun lover?"

"Rose and Della are not Huns," I said.

"I know." Iris Elizabeth put her arm around me. "But other people don't." She leaned closer, and I could smell her lavender sachet. "You see how they treat the Bolmans at school. Do you want to be shunned, too?"

Iris Elizabeth was right. A few people in other grades no longer talked to me, and they sometimes included me in the nasty names they tossed at Rose and Della.

For days, the newspaper was full of reports about soldiers, Allies, and Germans, dying from Spanish influenza. A call went out for additional nurses to serve overseas in the war zone, but all over the country, there were few nurses available. More and more deaths from influenza in New York, Boston, and other northern cities were reported.

However, influenza was not of interest in Miss Chambers' class. Much more exciting were the lacy white envelopes that lay in the center of the girls' desks after recess. Every girl, except Rose, Della, and Iris Elizabeth, had one. I picked mine up and quickly hid it in my pencil box while the other girls tore eagerly into theirs. Rose and Della kept their eyes on their readers, pretending not to see the commotion.

"Oh, it's for the tea," exclaimed Betty. "I can hardly wait till Sunday."

"I want everybody who got an invitation to come," Iris Elizabeth said.

Several girls giggled as they waved their invitations at Rose and Della. The look on Della's face stabbed at my heart.

"And," Iris Elizabeth went on, "you don't have to worry about getting to my house. My father will give every one of you a ride in the car."

"Hey, can I come, too?" asked Anthony Weaver, the smallest boy in the class.

"Me, too. I want to come. How about me?" came a chorus from the other boys.

"No, sillies." Iris Elizabeth smiled at first one boy and then another. "Teas are just for girls."

"I can't believe your father is going to drive around picking everybody up in the car," I said. "You know President Wilson said with the gas shortage there should be no driving of cars on Sundays."

Iris Elizabeth raised her eyebrows at me. "My father said nobody was going to tell him when he could and could not drive his own automobile. You don't have to ride, Annie."

Everybody kept talking until Miss Chambers walked into the room, and the hubbub was squelched. "Class, I have just heard some disturbing news," she said. "The Spanish influenza is not confined to cities at a distance from us. More and more cases have been reported in Mississippi, Tennessee, and Arkansas."

The next day three seats in our classroom were empty when Miss Chambers read from the newspaper that influenza had become an epidemic in Little Rock and was running rampant in Nashville. "Influenza seems to be on all sides of us," she said.

"I heard old Mr. Bolman has the flu," Billy Ray Barton said, and most of the class laughed.

"Is that true, Della?" Miss Chambers asked.

Looking miserably alone beside Rose's empty seat,

Della nodded. When Miss Chambers asked if Rose was sick, too, Della nodded again and kept twisting a strand of hair between her fingers.

"Now, boys and girls, I want you to be especially careful at this time," Mrs. Chambers said. "Stay away from people who are sneezing or coughing. If you feel sick, go to bed and stay there."

Della sat forlornly humped over her desk all day. As much as I wanted to, I could not bring myself to say anything to her. Iris Elizabeth was right. I did not want to be treated as a Hun lover.

Chapter Twenty-One

After lunch I felt so bad about not sitting with Della that I had a raging headache. By the time Iris Elizabeth and I left school, walking with the boys, even my back hurt. In the October sun, I should have been quite warm, but I was freezing cold, so cold that Robert took off his shirt for me to wear home. I kept thinking about Della walking all the way home with only Herman for company, and I began to shiver and could not stop.

"Annie," Iris Elizabeth shouted at me. "You haven't heard a word I've said."

My head hurt so bad I could hardly see her face.

"You're sick!" she said as she backed away from me.

I felt James and Robert taking my arms, and that was the last thing I remembered until I woke up in bed. My body ached all over, and my throat was on fire.

"Here, Annie," Mama said, "take this."

She poured a bad tasting liquid between my teeth and I had to swallow. "It's just aspirin water," she said. "Now go back to sleep and get well." Her cool hand felt good on my hot forehead.

The next time I woke, Mama was sitting in her rocking chair beside me, her chin in the air and her eyes closed. I drifted in and out of sleep, shivering under a mound of quilts. Mama was crying. Della was crying. I was crying. Why was everybody crying? My bones hurt. Mama's hands soothed the pain. My throat burned, and Mama made me drink. It hurt to swallow.

When I opened my eyes, Mama was still sitting beside me. Her eyes filling with tears, she leaned over and kissed my forehead. "Oh, Annie," she said. "I was so afraid I'd lose you. You have that nasty influenza, but you're going to be all right."

"What day is it, Mama?" My lips were so cracked and dry, I could hardly talk.

"It's Friday afternoon," she whispered. "Now don't talk. You'll wake Robert. Just lie here and rest, and I'll get you something to drink. You haven't eaten since lunch on Wednesday."

"I'm not hungry," I said, "just tired. Is Robert sick, too?" The top of Robert's head was sticking out of a bundle of bedcovers on Paul John's cot across the room.

"He came down with it yesterday," Mama said. "But his fever hasn't been as high as yours. Now be still." She went into the kitchen and began rattling dishes.

The noise made my head hurt, but not as bad as before. I had dozed off again when Mama came back with a glass. She held my head up and gave me a drink that burned my throat. "What is it?" I said.

"Just a little orange juice with egg white," she said. "I'm afraid to give you anything else."

I could not stay awake. Sleeping, I would wake shivering no matter how many quilts and blankets were piled on me. Then sweat would pour off, soaking my nightgown. Mama stayed with Robert and me, forcing liquid down our sore throats and sponging us off with water and alcohol. I don't think she slept at all.

Sunday evening I woke clear headed for the first time in days. I was hungry and ready to get out of bed. The parlor was dark with the shades down, and Robert was sitting up in bed, grinning at me. "You're a lazy thing," he said, "just lolling in bed."

"What about you?" It felt good to be able to think.

"Almost nobody was at school Thursday when I got sick," Robert said. "I guess everybody's got the flu."

Mama came in and collapsed in her chair. "I'm just thankful none of the rest of us has it," she said. "Mr. Bolman was deathly ill for a couple of days. William's been substituting for him at the cemetery."

Mama would not let Robert and me leave the parlor because she didn't want us spreading germs. We ate every bit of our scrambled eggs, applesauce, and milk pudding for supper, and Mama let us stay up and play checkers for a while.

"Robert," I said, "was Iris Elizabeth at school Thursday?"

"No, Katherine was the only girl in our class and just three of us boys," he said. "Why do you want to know?"

"Just wondering about the tea."

"Forget the dumb tea. You all were positively cruel to Rose and Della." Robert began coughing, covering his mouth with his hand. When he could breathe again, he said, "I'm ashamed of you."

"I didn't do anything."

"You should have stopped Iris Elizabeth."

My head was throbbing again with fever, and now Robert was mad at me.

The next morning I was ready to get out of bed and stay out. I changed from my nightgown into an old, faded dress. Then I rolled up the green shades that kept the parlor dark, and Robert sat up in bed.

"Where's Mama?" he asked.

Not a sound came from the kitchen. Mama was always in there bustling around. I walked in there wondering what was going on, and she was nowhere in sight.

A note from Daddy was on the table. "Annie and Robert," it said. "Take care of yourselves and your mama. She's sick now. I'm going to work. William is at the cemetery, and James is watching Paul John. Don't get around James and Paul John. We don't want them sick. The schools are closed."

Mama was in bed, pale and shivering. Robert grabbed blankets and quilts off our beds, and we piled them on Mama. I sponged her face and arms with alcohol water as she did for us. She continued to shiver while she slept, groaning under all the covers. I dissolved an aspirin in a little water and poured it into her mouth while Robert held her head. Then both Robert and I felt so weak we lay on Mama's bed, covered ourselves, and slept.

Mama's groaning woke me, and I made my wobbly legs carry me to the kitchen for more aspirin and water. Robert woke up and helped me get Mama to drink it.

Robert and I needed to eat to get our strength back so we could take care of Mama. I found some leftover cornbread and poured buttermilk from the icebox over it. I didn't feel like eating. I was tired from coughing and just wanted to sleep. Robert and I slept all afternoon on the bed with Mama, waking to sponge her off and give her aspirin.

Daddy came home from work early and told us everything in town was closed until the flu epidemic was over–all the schools, businesses, and churches. He sent Robert and me back to the parlor where we flopped on our beds. My head was aching again so I knew my fever was back.

Sometime later, Daddy called Robert and me to the kitchen to eat some soup he and James made. I didn't know he could cook. He never had before.

"I tried to get Aunt Loma to come over," Daddy said. "But her whole family, and Aunt Cal's, too, all have the flu. Mrs. Bolman's been taking care of Aunt Cal's family. I guess we're on our own."

The next day, things were worse. Every Davis in the house was sick, even Daddy. Robert and I were the only ones out of bed. We went from one to another piling on covers and giving aspirin. By ten o'clock in the morning, I was so tired and so scared my tears poured as much as Della's ever had as I sponged Paul John's arms. He looked so little and helpless.

"Annie," Robert said, taking the sponge from me as he handed me a glass of water to drink. "Stop a minute, and rest," he said. "We can do this. We have to."

I drained the glass of water and still felt thirsty. Everybody in the family was depending on the two of us to take care of them. And we were so weak we could hardly stand.

"We need a doctor or a nurse." I couldn't bear the

thought that the whole family was counting on Robert and me alone to care for them.

"Daddy told me all the doctors and nurses in the city, colored and white, have been organized to take care of the flu," Robert said. "All we have to do is telephone, and we'll get some help."

"I'll go over to the Robinsons' house to call. I'm glad they have a telephone," I said.

I still had on the dress I wore the day before so I just slipped shoes onto my bare feet and left.

Outside, the sun was shining through clouds, giving everything a sickly, greenish-gray tone. I dragged myself down the road. Nobody else was out, not one buggy or wagon in sight. When I finally reached the Robinson house, I barely had enough strength to crawl up the steps. I lay on the porch and knocked on the heavy door.

After what seemed an eternity, the door opened, and Iris Elizabeth stared down at me. "What are you doing here, Annie?" she said. "You're sick."

"We need a doctor." I leaned against an urn of ferns on the porch.

"Go home, Annie, and get in your bed," Iris Elizabeth said. "My parents said not to let anybody in the house while they're gone. We don't want to catch the influenza."

My true friend closed the door.

"Iris Elizabeth, call a doctor!" I tried to shout, but my hoarse voice was as weak as a whisper. It would never get through that thick door. I lay there trying to get enough strength to go home and hoping Iris Elizabeth would get us a doctor. I had to get back to see about the others. Holding onto the urn, I struggled to stand. Everything went black. When I came to, I managed to get down the steps and start home, praying as I went. *Oh, Lord, help us!*

Chapter Twenty-Two

The short distance home from the Robinsons seemed to take forever. Robert met me at the back door, his pale face taut with fear. "Daddy's on the floor, and I can't get him up," he said.

Daddy lay on the floor by his bed, burning up with fever and talking crazy. His face was paper white above his beard, and he was mumbling, "Edna... the babies...I can't..."

Robert and I struggled, tugging at Daddy's limp arms, but he was a big man, and we didn't have the strength to move him. So we poured more aspirin water in his mouth and left him on the floor, covered with blankets. He finally stopped mumbling and lay quiet.

Paul John began crying in the boys' room, and I went to soothe him. He was asleep, curled in a knot, whimpering softly. I sponged off his forehead and straightened his covers. He stopped crying.

Both James and William lay still as death in the bed they shared. I wiped their flushed faces, and William woke up. "Water," he croaked, so I poured a few sips into his mouth.

In the kitchen, Robert was dissolving aspirin in water. "I'm worried about Mama," he said, running his hand through his wiry hair that was already standing on end. He had dark circles under his eyes, and I knew he was as bone tired as I was.

"Me, too," I said. "Her breathing sounds funny and she coughs too much."

"Do you think Iris Elizabeth called a doctor?" he said.

I shook my head. I didn't know what Iris Elizabeth might do and didn't have time to think about it. "Nobody came," I said. "Are you hungry, Robert? We have to eat something to build up our strength."

"I know, but I'm not hungry."

I knew how he felt. I just wanted to sleep, but we had to take care of the others. We heated a jar of green beans and opened some canned tomatoes Mama put away for the winter. While we ate, we decided I would stay the night in the room with Mama and Daddy, and Robert would be with the boys.

Somehow, we made it through the night. In the morning we were mopping heads, pouring aspirin water down throats, and shifting covers from hot ones to cold ones when there was a knock on the back door.

Never had anybody looked so good to me as Mr. Bolman with a white sack on his back and a bucket of milk in his hand.

"Mr. Bolman!" I leaped at him, nearly knocking him down the steps. Thank the Lord! Help at last!

Robert pulled Mr. Bolman into the kitchen and slammed the door like catching a butterfly in a jar before it could flit away. We smiled for the first time in two days as Mr. Bolman set the milk on the table and pulled two loaves of bread from his bag.

"I stopped by to see if you are all right," he said.

"Where's your mother?"

"She's sick, real sick. Daddy and the boys are sick, too," I said.

"Daddy's on the floor," Robert added. "We can't get him up."

Mr. Bolman marched into the bedroom, scooped Daddy up off the floor like a huge rag doll, and plopped him on the bed beside Mama. For a little man, Mr. Bolman was amazingly strong, and he was just getting over being sick himself.

Daddy began thrashing about, talking again. "No, no, Edna. I need to…"

Mr. Bolman laid one hand on Daddy's forehead and one on Mama's. "Burning up with fever, both of them," he said. "You the only ones can walk?"

"Yes," Robert said. "We've been taking care of everybody."

"Terrible, terrible!" Mr. Bolman slowly shook his head. "I'll be back," he said.

Then he was gone, driving his wagon down the road.

Duty weighed on my shoulders like a lead coat, as Robert and I went from one of the sick to another as we had all night. One minute, they were hot to touch, shaking with fever, and the next they felt as cold and clammy as a dead fish. The worst thing was not knowing what to do. Neither of us had ever been around a really sick person before. The Davises were known to be as healthy as horses.

About midday I made some lumpy oatmeal and put in dried apples and sugar for Robert and me. Again, neither of us was hungry. We told each other we had to eat, and we ate silently, so tired we couldn't talk.

I woke with my spoon in my mouth and my face almost in my bowl. A rumbling sound like a couple of coal wagons on the road made me think a storm was coming. Robert raised his head from the table and looked about wildly as the rumbling turned into knocking. The back door opened, and a tall, thin man with black hair and a little mustache stepped into the kitchen.

"I'm Dr. Blumenfeld, checking to see if anybody here is sick with influenza," he said. He set a cardboard box of oranges on the table and opened his black doctor's bag. "Let me look at the two of you," he said coming toward me with a stethoscope in his hand. "Where are your parents?"

"Everybody's sick," Robert said. "We've been taking care of them."

"Don't look at us," I said. "The others are sick. Come see Mama." I led Dr. Blumenfeld into the bedroom where Mama and Daddy lay shivering under tons of cover.

Dr. Blumenfeld was wonderful. He gave Mama and the others some medicine to help them sleep comfortably and left cough medicine and quinine to use instead of aspirin. He told us to keep the windows open for air, but not to let it get cold in the sick rooms. We were to beat egg whites with orange juice and try to get everybody to drink it. He said Robert and I were doing everything right, and he told us how to schedule medicine, sponge-offs, and drinks so we could rest. He said if we didn't rest and get enough food, we'd be sick again, worse than ever, and not be able to help anybody.

Before he left, Doctor Blumenfeld told Robert and me to sleep while the rest of the house was asleep. I heard the back door close as I dozed off. When I woke, the parlor was dark. I stretched and huddled down under the covers for another quick snooze. Then the horror of the day came flooding back, and I jumped up. A light was on in the kitchen, and Robert was squeezing orange juice into a fruit jar.

"I have to see about Mama and the rest," I said grabbing the sponge and a pan of water. How could I have slept so long?

"Don't worry," Robert said. "I checked, and everybody's all right. James and William threw off their covers, and they want something to drink."

I cracked an egg and tried to let the white slide into a bowl while keeping the yolk in the shell to put in another bowl for scrambled eggs. I'd seen Mama do that a million times, but when I tried, part of the yolk went in with the white, the white ran down my arm, and shells got in both bowls. After fishing out the shells, I beat the whites with a fork until they were frothy and poured them into the juice Robert fixed for everybody.

In the boys' room, James and William were able to sit up enough to drink their mix, but Robert had to hold Paul John's head up while I spooned his into his mouth. When a spoonful didn't go down right, Paul John strangled, coughing and gasping for breath. Robert pounded his back, and I raised his arm up as I'd seen people do with choking babies.

"Mama, Mama," Paul John cried when he could breathe again.

"Mama's sick," I told him, rubbing his back the way Mama did mine. "We'll take care of you." *Poor little guy!*

I tucked the covers in around him and patted him until he dropped off to sleep.

Then we went to see about Daddy and Mama. Daddy drank all his juice and wanted more, but Mama only took a few sips of hers.

All of our patients seemed better, thanks to Dr. Blumenfeld, so we went back to the kitchen.

"Wonder what happened to Mr. Bolman," Robert said. "He said he was coming back."

As I stirred milk into the egg yolks to make scrambled eggs for Robert and me, I suddenly remembered. "The chickens! We forgot to feed the chickens!"

"I took care of them before you woke up," Robert said, "and Dandy, too."

After Robert and I stuffed ourselves with scrambled eggs and Mr. Bolman's bread covered with Mama's pear preserves, it was long past our usual bedtime. We knew we'd be up and down all night taking care of the sick ones. I cleaned up the kitchen while Robert carried the bedpan to the boys and Daddy.

Then I took care of Mama. Her face was pale, and she was still feverish, but she opened her eyes and patted my cheek as I straightened her bedcovers. "Go, rest," she whispered.

Chapter Twenty-Three

Robert and I settled down in the parlor after making one last round. I didn't think I would sleep and didn't know I did until I woke, hearing Daddy's cough.

Groping through the dark parlor, I made my way to the kitchen where I turned on the light to get the cough medicine. I spooned a dose into Daddy's mouth, and he patted my arm. "You and Robert are good nurses," he said before he dozed off again.

Mama's forehead was damp and cool when I felt it, and her breath came in short wheezes. I made sure she was covered and let her sleep.

After that, I only slept in short spurts between nursing bouts. Yet, at the first pink feathers of dawn, I felt I was ready to face anything. Nothing could be worse than the day before.

I had worn the same dress day and night since Mama got sick and never gave it a thought until now. What would Iris Elizabeth think? To my surprise, I didn't care what she thought. I cleaned up, put on another old faded dress, and finally had a chance to get the tangles out of my hair while everybody was still asleep.

When I went into the boys' room, William and James were awake, sitting up in bed.

"What have you got to eat?" James croaked at me

with a grin.

"Yeah," William said, "I'm starved."

"*Shh*! Don't wake Paul John," I said. "You two lie back down now. Be still and quiet while I get your breakfast." It wasn't often that I got to tell William or James what to do.

As I turned to leave, William reached out and swatted me on the rear and then laughed until he started coughing.

Daddy waved and smiled when he saw me at his door.

"Are you ready for breakfast?" I asked.

He nodded vigorously and put his finger to his lips to let me know I shouldn't wake Mama.

I made egg-white orange juice again, a pot of runny oatmeal, and scrambled eggs. I had decided to tackle milk gravy when a sleepy-eyed Robert appeared in the kitchen.

"Get yourself cleaned up before breakfast," I said.

He rubbed his eyes and yawned, "You sound just like Mama. Who made you the boss?"

I grinned at him. It felt good to be in control.

My gravy was one big, pale blob, but nobody cared. Everybody except Mama and Paul John ate all their breakfast, and Daddy said he didn't know I was such a good cook. I didn't either. Mama finished about half of her oatmeal and orange juice, and Robert was feeding Paul John the last of his oatmeal when we heard a wagon.

I hurried back to the kitchen with Mama's dishes, and through the window saw Dolly pulling the Bolman wagon into the yard. "Robert, Mr. Bolman's back," I said. "And Rose is with him!"

Mr. Bolman and Rose brought in more bread and a bucket of milk. "Thought you'd have plenty of eggs since you have chickens," he said. "Rose is here to help you. I'm taking this food to the other sick neighbors."

With his wagon still more than half full of bread, milk, and eggs, he drove off. Rose and I began cleaning up the mess I made with breakfast, and Robert worked with us.

"Daddy was bringing me over late yesterday to help you," Rose said. "But when we stopped at Aunt Lizzie's, we discovered that she and Uncle Tom were so sick they had to go to the hospital. We took them to a special hospital set up at Central High School for influenza."

"A hospital at the school!" Robert said.

"Yes. There're too many sick people for the regular hospitals," Rose said. "The newspaper said there are about ten thousand cases of flu in Memphis. Anyway, while we were there we saw Iris Elizabeth in a car. Turned out, it was Dr. Blumenfeld's car. Her parents were in the hospital. They came down with the flu when they ran out of gas and had to walk home."

"Walk home? Mrs. Robinson?" I couldn't imagine her tripping along the road in her fancy shoes.

"She had to. They couldn't get gas. They got sick on the way and some farmer put them in the back of his wagon, with his sick wife, and took them all to the hospital at the school.

"Serves them right for being out driving, wasting gas. I don't care where they'd been," Robert said.

"The doctor found Iris Elizabeth at home and didn't

want to leave her alone because she might get sick," Rose said. "You should have seen her. She was scared blue and speechless. Daddy said he'd take her home with us, and she never said one word about Germans or Huns."

"Did she go home with you?" I asked.

Rose laughed. "She climbed up on that wagon seat and sat between the two of us Huns like she was pleased to be there."

Robert and I had a good laugh at that.

"After all that, it was about midnight," Rose said, "and Daddy decided it was too late to come back over here. 'Robert and Annie can handle it. I know they can,' he kept saying. But he was worried about you."

"I guess we have handled it." Never before had I felt so close to my family or so glad to be a Davis.

"But we're happy you're here," Robert said. He awkwardly patted Rose's shoulder.

"How is Della?" I asked. "When I was sick, I kept seeing her cry. I wish I..."

"Don't worry about Della. She's fine." Rose gave me a hug, and I knew I was forgiven.

"It's time for everybody's medicine," I said. "Do you want to help?"

"That's why I'm here," Rose said.

William and James both got dressed and declared they could take care of themselves and Paul John if we would make sure they got some dinner.

Daddy said, "I feel so much better I'm getting up this afternoon. I can see after your mama."

As Rose and I gathered up dirty clothes and bedcovers to wash, I asked, "How is Iris Elizabeth taking everything?"

Rose smiled, her eyes twinkling as they hadn't for a long time. "You should have seen Miss Iris E this morning, dressed in Cousin Bertha's hand-me-down dress, carrying a bucket of milk with Della. You know Mother. Nobody can sit around doing nothing."

We both laughed so hard that I started to cough, and Robert had to know what was so funny.

The rest of that morning, Rose and I stayed on the back porch, washing piles of clothes, putting them through the wringer from the wash, to the rinse, and through the second rinse. Robert hung them out to dry, filling the clotheslines and draping them over fences. We brought the clothes and bedcovers in the minute they were dry and dumped them in the parlor to fold.

Then we cooked. The three of us together made a good dinner of mashed potatoes, ham, green beans, biscuits, and gravy. All of our patients came to the dinner table, except Mama, and even she said she was feeling better. Everyone still had fever off and on, so in the afternoon they all lay down to rest, while Rose, Robert, and I fixed supper. Rose showed us how to make peach cobbler from dried peaches.

When Mr. Bolman returned to get Rose, I hated to see her go, but she gave me a hug, and said, "Everything's going to be all right."

That's what I thought. The Davises were beating the flu, and after all he'd done to help people during the sickness, nobody could think anything bad about Mr. Bolman.

I gave Rose a peach cobbler to take home just as Mama would have. After Rose was gone and Robert was in bed, I sat in Mama's rocking chair with Dandy in my lap. The worst was over, and Robert was right. We could do it.

The next day, everybody was out of bed except Mama. A man stopped by to see Daddy and came back later with a load of lumber. Daddy immediately began sawing and hammering, stopping often to rest.

The undertakers had run out of coffins, and he was hammering together some rough boxes for flu victims. The epidemic was so bad that people weren't allowed to have funerals because gatherings of people would spread the flu.

There were so many to bury that the cemeteries didn't have enough workers. William started working at Forest Hill as soon as he was strong enough, and James helped Daddy build coffins.

Robert and I were still busy every day washing clothes, cooking, and taking care of Mama and Paul John. Paul John didn't seem sick any more, but he wanted Mama. One day he hung on me and cried and whined until Mama said, "Let him come in here to me."

When he heard that, he ran and climbed on Mama's bed, cuddled up with her, and went sound asleep. Mama wrapped one of his curls around her finger. Then she looked up at me, and smiled. "I've been so blessed," she said, "with five wonderful sons and the best daughter in the world. Sit by me for a minute, Annie."

She took my hand and pulled me down to sit on the side of the bed. "I am very proud of you, Annie."

A coughing spell racked her body, and she gasped for breath, pressing her fist into her chest, as I ran for the cough medicine. After a spoonful, she lay back, exhausted. "*Ooo*, that hurt!" she said.

I thought she was sleeping again when her eyes opened, and she said, "Annie, I love you! Don't you forget it." Mama had never said anything like that before. She wasn't one for saying what she felt. In spite of all my willfulness, she said she loved me.

Chapter Twenty-Four

By evening Mama was burning up with fever again, and Daddy sent for Dr. Blumenfeld. "Pneumonia," the doctor said, shaking his head. "She should be in a hospital, but they're so crowded I think you can take better care of her here at home. Give her alcohol rubs and hope the fever breaks. Continue the quinine, and be sure she gets enough water. I would stay but I have too many other patients in the same condition. I'll be back in the morning."

All of us were worried about Mama. Daddy sat by her bed while I fixed supper. After the boys and I cleaned up the kitchen, we stood by Mama's bed. Her skin was hot to touch.

"You all go on to bed now, and get your rest," Daddy said. "We don't want any of you getting sick again."

"But, Daddy," I said, "I want to stay with Mama. I'll take care of her."

"You get on to bed," Daddy said. "I can take care of your Mama."

The house was quiet that night, but I kept waking from terrible dreams. In one I was on the side of a steep hill when a huge bear came up behind me, his breath hot on my neck. The hill crumbled and I was sliding and tumbling down with the bear right behind me. Another time I thought a big, black monster that kept changing shapes was chasing me through the cemetery, coming closer and closer.

When I woke again, the gray light of early dawn was creeping in around the parlor's dark shades, and a beam of light flowed in through the kitchen door. Mama must be in the kitchen. No, she was sick in bed.

I found Daddy sitting at the kitchen table, his face haggard and full of shadows. "Morning, Daddy," I said as I leaned over his back and pressed my cheek to his. Above his beard, his face was cool against mine.

He absent-mindedly patted my arm and said, "Tell your brothers to come into the parlor."

That was strange, but I felt an urgency to do what he said without questions. When I passed Mama's room, I noticed the door was closed. We never closed doors. Daddy probably wanted the room quiet so she could sleep.

The boys were all awake, even Paul John. "Daddy wants you in the parlor," I said.

"Why?" James said.

"I don't know, but you'd better come now."

William swept up Paul John, and James and I followed them to the parlor where Robert sat on his cot.

As soon as we were all there, Daddy came in from the kitchen, looking like an old man, dazed and confused. "Your mama," he said softly. His head bowed to his chest, his hands covered his face.

"What about Mama?" James said.

Daddy just shook his head.

"Mama's passed away," William said, his voice flat and empty.

A cold numbness crept over me. I could hardly breathe. It couldn't be true that Mama was gone! I wanted to shriek and cry, but my eyes were dry. How could we do without her? I sat down on the sofa, and Paul John crawled into my lap. I wrapped my arms around his warm little body.

Daddy's sad eyes rested on each of us for a second or two before he walked out the back door, bent in sorrow. He trudged down the road, leaving me alone with my brothers.

William sat beside me on the sofa, his arm over my shoulder. "We have a lot to do." His voice cracked, and he swallowed hard. "Annie, can you get her ready? I'm going to dig her the best grave there ever was."

Numbly, I nodded. James took Paul John from me, and we all went together to see Mama. She was lying in bed as if she were asleep, a slight smile on her lips. Daddy had pulled the covers up under her chin, and she was a narrow ridge down the middle of the bed. It was true. Mama was gone.

I didn't know where to begin. Mama would never again tell me what to do. The boys were rattling around the kitchen as I stood gazing at Mama. She never had elegant furniture or fancy dishes. She didn't go to the theater or travel very far. The family was her life, and her serene face proved that she never regretted it. The only fine dress she'd ever had was her wedding dress. She kept it in layers of tissue paper at the bottom of the trunk at the foot of her bed. Her wedding dress would be her burial dress.

I sat in Mama's rocker, her white wedding dress spread across my lap. My finger traced the delicate flowers in the lace covering the satin bodice. With so much to do, I should be busy, but I sat.

Mr. Bolman's wagon, loaded with people, pulled up into the yard. Through the window I saw Daddy and Mr. Bolman unload a few pieces of smooth, dark, reddish brown lumber while Mrs. Bolman and the girls carried armloads of things toward the house.

Mrs. Bolman came in and set a bundle of food on the table. "Annie, you poor dear!" she said. She pulled me out of the rocker and pressed me against her ample bosom. She smelled like fresh air and Ivory soap.

Rose and Della were followed by another girl, a colored girl. Elvie! In Mrs. Bolman's embrace, I began sobbing and could not stop. She patted my back and said, "Now, Annie, don't you worry about a thing. We are all here to help. Aunt Cal sent Elvie since she had to go back over to the Robinsons. Child, what are you doing with your mother's wedding dress?"

Sniffling, I managed to stammer, "It's her burial dress."

"Oh, no, Annie. Edna was saving that dress for you," Mrs. Bolman said. "For your wedding. Let's find something else."

"No! I want her in this dress. It's the one lovely thing she has, and I won't take it away from her."

"If that's the way you feel. It's your decision, but I know Edna wanted you to have it," Mrs. Bolman said.

She sighed and looked around. "Well, let's get started. Girls, you can clean the parlor while I take care of Edna."

"I want to tend to Mama," I said.

"I know you do, Annie," Mrs. Bolman said, "and I

will help you. Have you thought about how to line that fancy coffin your daddy's making? He insisted on getting the finest mahogany, none of that rough pine for his Edna."

By mid-afternoon, the parlor was sparkling, thanks to Rose and Elvie. Della and Robert had kept Paul John outside most of the morning. Paul John didn't really understand what was going on. He wanted to be with Mama.

He and Della picked bouquets of flowers, wild asters and goldenrod mostly, and filled fruit jars with them and colorful fall leaves. Della had brought a bag full of graveyard ribbon, and she helped Paul John tie big bows around each jar of flowers for Mama.

Mama lay in her white burial dress on her bed waiting for her coffin while Daddy worked with a passion, sawing, gluing, and hammering. He didn't stop to eat a bite of the dinner Mrs. Bolman fixed for us. James worked with Daddy, sanding and sanding until that mahogany glowed with a satiny sheen.

Rose and Elvie made a beautiful pillow and liner for the coffin from the peach-colored dress Iris Elizabeth gave me. It was Mama's favorite. As I watched Rose and Elvie making tiny stitches in the satin, I wondered if I would ever be able to do that.

Having Elvie in the house again was a comfort. It was like all those years we hadn't seen each other didn't count. We were still two halves of the same whole.

In the evening, William came home and announced that Mama's grave was ready. Daddy was carving a rose in the lid of the coffin.

"The most beautiful coffin I've ever seen," Mr.

Bolman said as all the visitors piled into his wagon.

"Now if you need anything, just let us know," Mrs. Bolman said. "I hate to leave, but we have to take care of the animals."

I was glad for all the help, but relieved when the helpers were gone and just our family was left, all together for the last time, all but Richard. He would have a terrible shock when he came home.

We gathered in the parlor and sang some of the hymns that Mama loved. William read her favorite Psalm, the twenty-third. Mama was beautiful in her coffin, resting in peach and white, her work done.

Daddy closed and sealed the lid. He and the boys carried the coffin down Hernando Road to Forest Hill. Paul John and I followed, our arms loaded with wild flowers and fall leaves. It seemed right that only our family accompanied Mama to her grave beside Mary and the baby.

Chapter Twenty-Five

My world had changed. Without Mama, I was the woman of the house, responsible for meals and household chores. Daddy hired Elvie to come on Saturdays, and she didn't seem like paid help at all. I loved working with Elvie, but I missed Mama. At times, the slightest thing would remind me of Mama, and I could not hold back the tears.

The first Saturday Elvie came to work, we both felt a little strange. She stood just inside the back door, a pretty girl with dark hair pinned back and smooth skin the color of caramel candy. She unfolded one of Aunt Cal's white aprons, slipped it over her head, and wrapped it around herself at least three times.

"You can't wear that big thing," I said, taking two of Mama's aprons out of the worktable drawer, one for Elvie and one for me.

She grinned as we put on Mama's aprons. We were still exactly the same size. "I can do whatever you want, Miss Annie," she said.

That struck me funny, Elvie calling me Miss Annie. "You can't call me Miss Annie," I said when I could stop laughing.

"I have to," Elvie said. "That's what Mama told me."

"I won't answer if you do. We're friends."

"You know coloreds and whites can't be friends. Mama's told me that often enough."

"She's told me too, but you're still my friend," I said. "You know Aunt Cal and Mrs. Bolman are friends."

"They may be, but neither one of them would ever say it," Elvie said. "Mrs. Bolman was at our house a lot when we were all sick. I'd wake up, and there she was with a cool wet cloth on my forehead. But no matter how close Mama and Mrs. Bolman are, Mama always calls her Mrs. Bolman."

"Call me whatever you like," I said. "You want me to call you Aunt Elvie?"

Elvie looked startled, and then she burst out laughing. We laughed so hard and so long we could hardly breathe. After that, the strangeness between us was gone, and we were just glad to be together again.

After the first week of November, the worst of the flu epidemic was over. Our neighborhood had been hit hard, and a lot of families suffered losses. Miz Lizzie was now a widow, and a number of desks were empty when school reopened. Charlie Dodd with his teasing and his mischief was gone. I cried for Charlie. He was too young and full of life to die.

The newspapers carried long lists of soldiers killed and injured in the war. Peach pits and other seeds were still needed for gas masks. While the schools were closed, the Liberty League picked up the seed collections, and no class marched in the parade as winners. The good news was that our soldiers in Europe had fought the Germans so hard they were ready to surrender.

One evening a few weeks after Mama's burial, Mrs. Robinson and Iris Elizabeth came to see me. To offer their condolences they said. I had not heard a word from either of them since I went to their house to use the telephone. Iris Elizabeth had not come back to school.

As I cleared away the supper dishes, Mrs. Robinson parked herself in a chair, her taffeta skirt billowing onto the bare wooden planks of the kitchen floor. She belonged in our house about as much as one of her Tiffany lamps was fit for an outhouse. "Annie," she said, "the Orpheum is presenting a special show to celebrate the end of the war. We want you to go with us Friday evening."

My heart leaped with excitement. To see a show in the gold and crystal splendor of the Orpheum after being in the house for so long with so much to do! But Paul John would not go to sleep until I lay down beside him for a little while every night. And I always had the kitchen to clean up for the next day.

"Annie, I haven't seen you lately." Iris Elizabeth gave me one of her most beguiling smiles. She eyed my faded dress and tousled hair. "You could wear that ice-blue silk dress. It would be perfect with the pink one I'm wearing."

I had missed Iris Elizabeth and felt myself falling under her spell again. But she had never come once to see about me, not even when Mama died. Her parents had been home for a long time with Aunt Cal to care for them. Elvie told me Mrs. Robinson was never sick. She had stayed with Mr. Robinson in the hospital, demanding service, until the doctors kicked them out to make space for the truly ill.

"I don't believe I can..." I said. I didn't want to go anywhere with the Robinsons.

Daddy, reading his newspaper after supper as usual, looked up at me and said, "You think we can't get along without you for a little while, Annie? Of course, she'll go. Appreciate you asking her, Mrs. Robinson."

Friday evening I felt as uneasy with the Robinsons as I had when I first got to know them. Nothing seemed real. We were all actors on a stage, and when the evening was over, we would stop pretending and go back to our real selves.

One of their friends, a tall distinguished man, said, "Edward Robinson, you have a lovely family."

Mrs. Robinson raised her eyebrows at Mr. Robinson and gave a little nod. "The girls are beautiful together," she said, "like a pair of exquisite figurines."

After dinner and the theater, Iris Elizabeth walked to my door with me while her parents waited in the car. "Wouldn't you like to have evenings like this all the time?" She gave me a quick hug. "We have a surprise for you later."

I could not imagine what the surprise could be. Maybe another glittering night of make-believe.

The next evening after supper, Mrs. Robinson and Iris Elizabeth appeared again. When Daddy closed his newspaper and rose from the table, Mrs. Robinson said, "Wait, Mr. Davis. It's you we came to see."

"Really, now." Daddy took out his pipe and held it in both hands. "What would you two fine ladies have to do with me?"

That's what I wanted to know. Neither Mrs. Robinson nor Iris Elizabeth had ever given Daddy the time of day. Iris Elizabeth caught my eye and gave me the most radiant smile ever.

"Mr. Davis, it's about your daughter," Mrs. Robinson said.

"What about her?" The wrinkles across Daddy's brow deepened. "What's Annie done?"

"Oh, nothing at all, Mr. Davis, except be a perfectly charming, lovely young girl. You should be very proud of Annie."

Daddy gave a short nod and waited.

Mrs. Robinson fingered the jeweled brooch at her neck. "As a father who wants the best for his daughter, I know you'll agree to the proposition my husband and I offer."

"What are you talking about?" Daddy demanded.

"In the very near future we will be returning to our home up north," Mrs. Robinson said. "Iris Elizabeth has developed quite an attachment to Annie. We all have. I know you would not want to keep your lovely daughter here performing menial household tasks when she has the opportunity to know the finer things in life with us."

Daddy erupted. "What are you saying, woman? That you want to take Annie away from me?" He jammed his pipe into his mouth and walked out into the night.

Mrs. Robinson and Iris Elizabeth were twin pictures of shock. With wide eyes and open mouths, they looked like a pair of surprised fish. Iris Elizabeth recovered first. "Talk to him, Annie. You can bring him around."

They actually thought I would leave my family and go with them! Mama was right. I did not want to be like Mrs. Robinson. She never gave one thought to Daddy's or my feelings. "Iris Elizabeth, I could never leave my family," I said.

"But, dear," Mrs. Robinson said, "think of the opportunities you would have with us. You would become a lady of culture and someday meet a nice young man. You and Iris Elizabeth make a striking appearance, and you'd be showered with attention wherever we go."

Appearance. That's all she thought about. What about Paul John and his warm, little arms around my neck? Robert. James. William. Richard would be home soon. And Daddy. Daddy depended on me. They were my world, not the staged elegance and glamour of the Robinsons.

"Annie, don't you want to be my friend forever?"

Iris Elizabeth didn't know the meaning of friendship.

I gazed at a spider web hanging from the corner of the ceiling near the back door. Elvie and I had missed it this morning.

"After all we've done for you," Mrs. Robinson fumed. "Such an ungrateful girl! Come, Iris Elizabeth, the sooner we're out of this town, the better I'll like it."

I stood in a daze, hearing Mrs. Robinson and Iris Elizabeth storm across the back porch and down the steps. The thought that I'd never see either of them again passed over me like a spring rain washing away mud and debris from a paved road. I felt new and free with no more cause to pretend.

Paul John burst into the kitchen. "What did Iris Elizabeth and her mama want?" he asked. "Where'd Daddy go?"

"I don't know where Daddy went." I grabbed him and hugged him tight, breathing in his healthy, little boy smell. "The Robinsons didn't want anything that I could see. Now let's get you cleaned up for bed."

When Paul John was in bed and sleeping after his prayers and a story, and the clean kitchen was ready for tomorrow's breakfast, I sat in Mama's chair and rocked. In the quiet house, my loneliness and aching for Mama was much worse than the most horrible headache. The murmur of voices from my brothers and the neighbor boys on the porch soothed the ache.

Later my brothers were all asleep in their room, and I was dozing in Mama's chair when Daddy flung open the door.

Seeing me, his face brightened with a little smile as he closed the door. "Annie, I'm glad you're still up."

He pulled a chair from the table and sat close beside me. "I don't know how to start. I shouldn't have run out and left you here like that. I did the same thing when your mother passed, and I'm ashamed of myself," he said.

He took my hand in his strong carpenter hands, rough from working outside, and held it gently. "I want you to listen to me, Annie. I've been walking and pondering. Your mother was always afraid the Robinsons would take you away from us, and she hated the thought of you growing up to be like that girl and her mother. I do want you to have an easier life than your mother did. I want you to have nice things and enjoy life. But, Annie, not with the Robinsons."

He took a deep breath and put his finger over my lips when I started to speak. "No, listen to me. I can forgive most anything, but what Edward Robinson did to John Bolman is beyond all I've ever seen. He tried to destroy the Bolman family, accusing John of treason, just to make himself look big. Even after those two drifters from St. Louis said they hatched their harebrained plot to sink the barge after drinking moonshine half the night, Robinson continued to make accusations against John. I cannot understand that. And I will not let you go with the Robinsons. You belong here with me and your brothers."

"Daddy, I've already told Mrs. Robinson I wouldn't go with them," I said. "And she's really put out with me."

"Oh, Annie, you're just like your mother." He pulled me out of the rocker and onto his lap. "I should have known you had too much sense to be taken in by the Robinsons."

Chapter Twenty-Six

A week later, Paul John romped with Dandy through the brown, gold, and red leaves covering the backyard. James and Robert, digging the last of the potatoes, had chased them out of the garden.

In the kitchen, Miz Lizzie kept a sharp eye on Paul John through the window. He stayed with her every day while we were at school. Saturdays and weeknights she came over to help me cook, usually staying for supper. I don't know if it helped Miz Lizzie or us more. She was bound to be lonely in that big house.

Elvie and I were shelling dried corn from the garden to use in the winter. Rose, Della, and Miz Lizzie had come to help. We filled blue Mason jars with golden corn and put them on the shelves over the kitchen worktable with Mama's canned tomatoes and green beans. We had filled four flour sacks with corn, and a wooden cask for the chickens was nearly full.

Elvie scooped up several ears of corn from a bushel basket on the floor and piled them in the center of the table. Della and I grabbed the same one, looked at each other, and began giggling.

"Annie, do you miss Iris Elizabeth?" Della asked.

"Maybe a little," I said, "but don't you think all of us here shelling corn is more fun than that dress-up tea party she planned?"

"Definitely!" Rose said. "Why do you think the Robinsons left town in such a hurry?"

"William told me it was because even when all the people were dying from the flu," I said, "nobody would buy tombstones from Mr. Robinson."

Elvie nodded. "My mama says the Robinsons were not so rich. They moved away without paying her what they owed."

"No!" Miz Lizzie was shocked. "This neighborhood is much better off without the Robinsons."

"I guess we'll just have to be ignorant, uncouth rurals without them trying to change us all into high-class city ladies," Rose said with a wry smile.

"That's all right with me." I no longer had the slightest wish to live as Mrs. Robinson did. "I can be myself. Some evenings, our whole family goes outside for a game of tag, even Daddy. And nobody tells me to act like a lady. Right now, there's nowhere I'd rather be than here in the kitchen with my true friends."

The End

Meet the Author:

Grace E. Howell has always been an avid reader, and she still says, "I want to be a writer when I grow up." A former teacher and school librarian, she loves sharing books and stories with young people. Her writing has been in several magazines and anthologies, and she is now an editor for a national monthly periodical. *True Friends*, her first novel, is a story she had to write after hearing so much about the time of the Great War and the flu epidemic from family and friends who lived through it.

Ms. Howell grew up in the *True Friends* neighborhood and lives with her husband in Memphis, Tennessee. They have one daughter, three sons, and three grandchildren. As a master gardener, Grace volunteers at the Memphis Botanic Garden, landscapes new homes for Habitat For Humanity, and is working to restore the Lee House gardens in historic Victorian Village.

Also available from Echelon Press Publishing

Pretty, Pretty (*Young Adult Mystery*) K.C. Oliver

Quinn and Holly have landed the summer job of a lifetime; working in *Hawaii!* With great weather, beautiful scenery, and cute guys...it's a job to die for...literally. But with the help of new friend, Jaxon, they begin to uncover the horror behind the mysterious hotel. Only someone or something doesn't want them to learn the truth, and will stop at nothing to make sure that the only place they will be taking any secrets; is to their *graves!*

$9.99   ISBN 1-59080-253-5

Trails of the Dime Novel (*Western Adventure*) Terry Burns

Danger and excitement...In the late 1800's the imagination of a nation was fueled by the wonder of Dime Novels. Gunfights and showdowns...Rick Dayton is headed west to write the beloved stories only to find himself living them instead. The making of legends...Travel across the west with him as every new adventure offers another novel in the journey of a lifetime.

$13.99   ISBN 1-59080-386-8

Anna Chase and the Butterfly Girls (*Fantasy for Young Readers*) Jadan B. Grace

Anna Chase is thrilled to share the tales of the Butterfly Girls with her young daughter, Brandy. Stories of another time and place offer solace to the lonely heart of the young widow as she relives the triumphs and tragedies of the beautiful winged creatures. Day by day, Anna tells the story of the exquisite Lady Willow and handsome Baron of Butterfly Haven who triumph over drought and devastation.

$10.99   ISBN 1-59080-083-4

The Dreamer (*Fantasy for Young Readers*) Scott Matheson

It's bad enough being twelve years old, but when you're scrawny, and painfully shy, life is torture. To escape, William spends hours each day daydreaming, lost in the safe world of his imagination. Enter the Guardian of the Great Wall.

While on this magical adventure, William will fight incredible evil while discovering incredible truths about himself.

$14.99   ISBN 1-59080-235-7